For Matilda with love
P. F.

First published 2020 by Walker Books Ltd, 87 Vauxhall Walk,
London SE11 5HJ

2 4 6 8 10 9 7 5 3 1

Text © 2020 Polly Faber
Illustrations © 2020 Sarah Jennings

The right of Polly Faber and Sarah Jennings to be identified as author and illustrator respectively of this work has been asserted by them in accordance with the Copyright, Designs and Patents Act 1988

This book has been typeset in Palatino

Printed and bound in Great Britain by CPI Group (UK) Ltd, Croydon, CR0 4YY

British Library Cataloguing in Publication Data: a catalogue record for this book is available from the British Library

ISBN 978-1-4063-8900-5

www.walker.co.uk

MIX
Paper from
responsible sources
FSC® C020471

PRIMA DONNA PONY

POLLY FABER

illustrated by **SARAH JENNINGS**

WALKER BOOKS

CHAPTER ONE

"Ding-dong! Ding-dong! Ding-dong!" The doorbell rang insistently.

Rose paused halfway through buttering her toast and called upstairs, "Mum! Dad? There's someone at the door."

"At this time of the morning? Go and see what they want will you? Dad's in the shower and I can't find the file I need anywhere."

"Do I have to?"

"Please Rose. It'll only be the post or something. Have you eaten?"

"Yeth," mumbled Rose through a mouthful of toast.

The doorbell was still ringing. She wandered down the hallway shedding crumbs and peered through the bubbly glass of the front door. Rose frowned. There wasn't just someone at the door. There were loads of people. She looked behind her hopefully for rescue but none appeared. Rose took a deep breath and opened the latch.

A flurry of camera flashes went off in her face. Startled, Rose tried to shut the door, but a beaming woman thrust her foot in the gap. "Rose Steggles? Are you Rose Steggles?" she asked.

"Yes," said Rose uncertainly. She gave up the battle with the door and let the woman push it wide open. A sea of faces grinned at her. There was a television camera recording her too. Rose froze.

"Congratulations Rose! Congratulations indeed! You're our WINNER!"

A cheer went up. There was a popping noise and confetti scattered all over the front step and down the neck of Rose's school blazer.

"Winner?" repeated Rose, still frozen.

"Winner?" repeated Rose's mum, appearing at her shoulder, briefcase packed, ready to do her usual run for the train.

"Winner? I've always known our Rose was that. Great! What's she won?" asked Rose's dad, also appearing, still wet from the shower and wrapped in a small towel. He took in the large audience and cameras on the doorstep. "I'll get my clothes on." He dashed back up the stairs.

Rose's mind was blank. What had she won? She couldn't remember entering any competitions. Unless ... no. That was impossible. Everyone had entered that one. She couldn't have...

"Congratulations Rose!" the woman said again. "I'm Davina McKitterick, Head of PR at the Good For You Breakfast Cereal Company. Hundreds of thousands entered but we picked you! You got all the answers right and we loved your slogan – shorter and snappier than most, I can tell you." Davina rolled her eyes before continuing with a brighter smile, "Yes! It's really true and it's time to meet your prize…"

She swung her body to one side and indicated up

the garden path to where a lorry was parked. The crowd parted. The television camera focused on a ramp being lowered from the back of the lorry.

"You're the owner of a PONY, Rose Steggles! Meet Maltie Delight himself!"

Rose's prize stepped out. It *was* a pony. The crowd gasped. The pony stopped, took in his audience, and shook out his magnificent mane for their benefit.

The crowd let out a long, impressed, "Aaaah!"

This was not just any pony. Maltie Delight was the most beautiful pony anyone could ever have imagined. He had an almost pure white coat with just the faintest dappling of grey over his broad chest and hindquarters. He had a long flowing mane and tail that sparkled in the early morning sunlight as if they were made out of fine silver thread. His dark, noble eyes were fringed with eyelashes so long and thick it looked as if the pony was wearing mascara. All that was missing for him to be mistaken for a real-life unicorn was the horn.

A thick powder-blue satin sash hung around the pony-corn's neck. It read "Congratulations! You've Won Maltie Delight!" in big letters and, in smaller letters underneath, "Maltie Delight is a trademark of the Good For You Breakfast Cereal Company."

"Come on Rose! Come on! Come and meet your prize!" Davina grabbed hold of Rose by the elbow and practically pulled her down the garden path. "Hard to take in I realise. All your dreams come true at once eh?" She turned to a thin man by her side.

"Simon, get this toast out of shot and find the girl a bowl of Malties super quick pronto." Rose found herself parted from her first breakfast and handed a bowl filled with a second one. "That's it! Take the rope! Smile for the cameras Rose! Smile!"

Rose held the rope awkwardly and did as she was told. Maltie Delight, who was evidently practised in front of the press, dropped his head to show off his lovely long nose and peeked out winningly from behind his billowing fringe.

"Turn this way Rose," called one of the camera people. "Can you eat a spoonful of cereal too?"

Rose found holding a pony for the first time, smiling and manipulating a spoon of cereal all at once was tricky. She didn't even like cereal. She got in a tangle and spilled milk all down her blazer. Rose noticed Maltie Delight staring at the mess she'd made with what appeared to be disdain.

Her parents had finally absorbed the news and came rushing down the path. "A pony? What do you mean Rose has won a pony? We've nowhere to keep a pony!" Rose's dad, who had now got his clothes on, began interrogating Davina.

"You could put him in your shed Dan. Won't be needing your lawnmower any more!" joked Mr Ahmed from next door, who had come to join the crowd like so many of their other neighbours.

"Mr Steggles, wonderful to meet you. No need for sheds – don't you worry about a thing. It's all taken care of," soothed Davina, grasping Rose's dad by the hand and pumping his arm up and down. "Lucky, lucky Rose hasn't only won Maltie Delight. She's won a complete livery care package at your local stables too. We'll be taking care of all stabling costs."

"But Rose doesn't know how to ride!" objected Rose's mum.

Davina's eyebrows lifted slightly. "Doesn't know *yet*! She's also won full riding kit and one-to-one tuition to teach her all she needs to know. And we'll even send her on a residential riding holiday. Maltie Delight is a very well-schooled pony, quite used to crowds and traffic and all sorts of situations he's had to face for filming. He's an excellent choice for a beginner like Rose."

"But I thought you didn't like ponies? I thought you were scared of them?" Rose's mum looked at Rose, her eyes questioning.

Rose flushed red. "Mu-um! I'm not scared now. Maybe I used to be, a little, but that was years ago." She gulped and glanced across at Maltie. She tried not to picture the teeth of the Shetland pony who had pinched her ice cream on holiday once. Or the rolling eyes of the big black horse at the farm by Grandma's house who always chased her along the other side of the fence when she cycled past. Or the enormous clattering hooves of the carthorse at the fete parade that had only missed landing on her feet by millimetres. At least Maltie Delight seemed more interested in posing for the cameras than in Rose or her cereal. And – she risked a look at the pony's feet – his hooves were positively dainty.

Rose's mum shrugged. "If you're sure? Well then, how exciting!" She looked at her phone. "Help; I'm late for work. So sorry Rose, I'm going to have to run..."

Rose's dad put an arm round her shoulders and grinned. "It is exciting! It's brilliant. Imagine! Our

Rose the winner out of all those entries. What was your slogan, love?"

"I didn't think it'd win," said Rose. She looked at Maltie Delight; her prize, her ... pony. "I didn't think it had the teeniest chance."

Her head was spinning. Whatever her mum said, Rose did like ponies. She liked them in distant fields, seen dreamily from the window of a car or train. She liked them in books and films and on posters and drawn in the margins of exercise books. But she'd never ridden one. In fact, since the ice-cream incident (a whole mint choc chip cornet! Gone in ONE MOUTHFUL!), she'd never been close enough to even pat one.

Putting down the cereal bowl, Rose reached out cautiously to stroke the pony's beautiful grey neck. Maltie Delight blew out his nostrils in a slightly dismissive way but accepted her stroke. He turned his head and examined his sash. It was twisted. He shook his body so that the sash hung straight again.

"But you did win!" said Davina chirpily. She turned to Rose's parents. "If one of you will just sign this contract with the terms and conditions then we can leave you in peace. The lorry will take Maltie Delight down to the stables now so we can all get on with our day. Miss Pickford at Plum Orchard Riding Stables will be expecting you after school Rose. She'll start you off on your new life as a pony owner!"

"I should read that contract," said Rose's mum, rummaging in her pocket for glasses, but Rose's dad was already signing it happily.

"We're horse owners!" he said. "Who'd have thought it? Must say I've always quite fancied talking about my own nag. You'll be winning a gold medal in the Gymkhana Olympics before we know it Rose!"

"Yeah right Dad," said Rose. She didn't know much about ponies but she did know there was no such thing as a Gymkhana Olympics. And even if there had been, Rose knew she wasn't the sort of person to win a medal. She had never won anything. Except ... now she had! Everything still felt like a dream. How could she have won a pony? What would they say at school?

The cameras were packing up and the crowd were peeling off back to their homes and cars. Feeling braver, Rose put her hand back on Maltie Delight's neck. It was warm and silky smooth.

"Hello Maltie Delight," she said formally. "Pleased to meet you."

Maltie Delight didn't look at her. His attention was caught by the shiny paintwork of Mr Ahmed's well polished BMW.

Rose watched the pony. He appeared to be examining his reflection. He gave a little snort and his mane cascaded down his neck in a rippling wave. It seemed to please him. He swung his head round and did it again, all the while keeping one of his noble dark eyes firmly locked on the mirror-like car windows. Rose giggled. Her new pony was very, very handsome. And he didn't half know it.

CHAPTER TWO

"ROSE STEGGLES WON! ROSE STEGGLES WON THE MALTIE DELIGHT COMPETITION!" Lola Riley shouted it out to the whole school as Rose filed into the hall for assembly. Rose winced. Used to keeping a low profile, she'd hoped she might be able to keep her win a secret. She'd forgotten that her neighbours had been watching in the crowd that morning.

"NO talking in assembly, you know the... Really? Rose Steggles?" exclaimed Mr Haverstock from the stage. The headmaster scanned the rows until he spotted Rose, flushed crimson and trying to melt down into her chair. Her classmates were gasping and nudging each other. Mr Haverstock squinted at Rose in confusion. "Did you, Rose? You won that pony?"

Maltie Delight was famous – and so was the competition to win him. For over fifty years he'd been on the television advertising the crunchy nuggets of his namesake breakfast cereal. Of course, it hadn't been the same Maltie Delight all that time. Every few years, in a piece of publicity genius, the pony was "retired" to a child through a competition. Practically every child in the country bought a packet of the cereal, completed a spot-the-difference and wrote a tie-breaker slogan.

Rose nodded quickly at Mr Haverstock. She could hear a buzz of voices building around her.

"That girl won Maltie Delight? How did SHE win? Who is she even anyway? That is SO unfair!"

"I don't believe it. I refuse to believe it. Do you know how long I've been having riding lessons for? I wrote six pages about why they should choose me. Double-sided."

"I bet she doesn't know anything about ponies! What made them pick her?"

"ENOUGH CHATTER," said Mr Haverstock. "Well I never! Stand up for a round of applause Rose!" He beamed at her pointedly until Rose was forced to get to her feet for some half-hearted clapping. "How very very lucky you are! I wonder; how many other people here entered the Maltie Delight competition?"

Every single hand in the room went up, including the teachers'. Even Flynn Simpson, who was really allergic to all animals, raised his hand. He caught Rose looking at him and scowled. "I was going to sell the pony and fly to the Bahamas. My skin always clears up on a sunny beach."

"Why don't you share your winning slogan with us Rose?"continued Mr Haverstock. "We'd love to know your secret!"

Rose looked around hopelessly for an escape route. A sea of cross faces stared at her, waiting.

"It was... I wrote..." She faltered, her voice whispery. She hated being the centre of attention.

"Go on!" said Mr Haverstock. "Speak up!"

Rose coughed and tried again. "I mean... I just put..."

BRRRRRRRRRIIIIIIIIIIIIIIIIIIIINGGGGGGGGGGGG!!!

There couldn't have been a better timed fire alarm if Rose had burned the toast in the staffroom herself.

Everyone shoved back their chairs and rushed out into the playground and Rose breathed a sigh of relief.

There was no hope of fading back into her usual invisibility. For the rest of the day Rose found herself pointed at and whispered about wherever she went. Tash Ramirez, one of the popular girls, drew up her chair at lunch and said, "Hello Rose. I've been meaning to tell you that your hair is looking cute; you should always wear it down. Have you ever thought about dyeing it a better colour? And changing your shoes? And your skirt? I know! Why don't you come over to my house this weekend for a makeover? I could even make you look pretty! And afterwards you could thank me by taking me to the stables and..." she paused for breath and opened her eyes wider, "... I could ride your pony? Maybe I could borrow him for a while."

Rose smiled politely and didn't point out that Tash still hadn't returned her yellow highlighter that she'd borrowed two years ago.

Rose's usual dependable school allies – her fellow non-sporty, non-clever, non-glamorous, nonentities

– were off with her. She'd broken their unspoken pact by having something interesting happen. Everyone said the same thing to her, with varying degrees of bitterness: "You do realise you're the luckiest lucky person who has ever lived, don't you?"

By the time Rose's dad dropped her off at Plum Orchard Riding Stables that afternoon and Rose saw Maltie Delight saddled up and waiting for her in the yard, she was exhausted. And she was really uncomfortable.

To try to make herself look the part, Rose had changed into her new riding gear. It was all two sizes too large. The shiny leather riding boots were stiff and dug into her white jodhpur-clad shins when she walked. Her top half was swamped by a body protector and covered by a tweed hacking jacket that bunched up on her neck and shoulders and dangled down below her fingertips. And her fingers couldn't move because they were inside too-big riding gloves. Rose had never realised how heavy and hot riding gear could feel. It was like being the rusty Tin Man from *The Wizard of Oz*. The only good thing was the outfit made her less worried about being bitten by pony teeth. Even a starving lion would find chomping through so many layers a problem.

"Here's our big winner Rose kitted out ready for her first lesson. I'm Dan Steggles. We're all new to ponies – we know nothing!" Rose's dad held out his hand for the owner of Plum Orchard, Miss Pickford, to shake. The riding instructor smiled at him thinly but ignored his hand. Instead, Miss Pickford looked Rose up and down and gave a small nod of approval.

"Very suitable." Miss Pickford was wearing a similar outfit to Rose, although hers fitted better. "Welcome to Plum Orchard. I will make a rider of you, you fortunate child. Your horse is certainly showy but apparently he's a well-schooled animal." She gestured to Maltie Delight who was being held by a tall blonde girl. The girl smiled at Rose and her dad and patted Maltie Delight as Miss Pickford continued, "You are to have the great privilege of an hour of my undivided attention every day. You are very very lucky indeed.

Your seat will be second to none by the time I've finished with you."

"Thank you," said Rose, gulping. Her seat? Was she going to be turned into a chair?

"I'm Carolyn," said the blonde girl."I work here and I'll be looking after Maltie Delight. Have you ever ridden before Rose?"

Rose shook her head. She looked again at Maltie Delight. He was causing quite a stir in the yard. People were gathered in clusters admiring him and taking pictures with their phones. Maltie clearly knew exactly what was going on because he was tipping his heels and twisting his neck; adjusting his posture so his fans could get his best angles.

"I used to be scared of ponies," Rose admitted. "When I was younger. Much younger obviously. Much much younger. I'm not nervous now. Not at all. Uh-uh."

Rose felt her dad give her a squeeze around the shoulders.

"You're excited aren't you Rosie-Pose?" There was a note of doubt in his voice.

Rose looked at him and then smiled at Carolyn and Maltie Delight. She was excited. "Yes! Thank you for looking after him. I don't know anything about that either I'm afraid."

"I'll teach you," said Carolyn. "When you're ready. I know you've got a lot to take in."

"Enough chit-chat," said Miss Pickford, swiping a riding crop against her boots. "Lead him to the indoor school and get this child mounted."

Rose's first ever riding lesson began with a blur of

tangled leather straps and buckles being hauled up and down as she was shown where to put her feet and hands and Maltie's saddle was adjusted. Once on top, Rose felt like she'd been plonked in the pilot seat of a jet plane and told to prepare for take-off. She wanted to slide down and run away but Miss Pickford was already bellowing instructions. The riding instructor was even scarier than Maltie Delight: "Gather those reins! Keep your feet in the stirrups! Look between his ears! Keep contact with his mouth!"

Miss Pickford stood in the middle of a large woodchip-covered arena and Carolyn led the pony round and round while Rose slid about high up on the saddle and tried to understand what she was supposed to be doing. It all made little sense. How was Rose supposed to "keep contact" with Maltie's mouth? His mouth was miles away.

"Sorry. I'm useless," she muttered to Carolyn.

"You're doing fine," whispered Carolyn. "Miss Pickford's bark is worse than her bite. It gets easier."

At last the hour was over. Rose slithered off Maltie's back and into a jelly-like heap on the ground.

So that was riding? Every bit of her ached. Her prize had left her multicoloured with bruises.

"Saddle sore?" asked Carolyn with a sympathetic smile. "I'll untack Maltie and brush him down. Get home and have a bath and we'll see you tomorrow."

Rose opened her mouth to say perhaps she could help brush Maltie down, but the words didn't come out in time. Carolyn was already leading the pony off through the yard and Maltie Delight didn't look back. Rose turned away. She'd only have made a mess of helping, anyway.

That evening Rose ran herself a bath, lay back in the bubbles and stared at the ceiling. She'd won a pony! She couldn't believe it was true. She must be the luckiest lucky person in the world.

Rose tried to block out a familiar voice that intruded into her head. This voice whispered that Maltie Delight was the unluckiest pony. Because why had the competition judges chosen someone like Rose to be his owner?

CHAPTER THREE

"Are you a rider or a sack of potatoes?" Miss Pickford bellowed. The riding instructor didn't expect a response, but bouncing about on yet another circuit of sitting trot Rose knew that even after six weeks of lessons the answer was definitely potatoes.

Miss Pickford squinted at Rose, pursed her lips and sighed heavily. "I can do no more with you today. Bring him in at marker C and dismount. Tomorrow we shall remove your stirrups and reins and carry on with sitting trot. Your seat must be much more secure if you are to make any progress."

Rose slithered off her pony gratefully. Her seat was mashed potato. Slipping Maltie's reins over his head, she took a deep breath and hobbled towards the yard. As usual, a group of confident riders were there, chatting and picking out their ponies' hooves. Rose knew what would come next. So did Maltie – he was already pulling forwards with more enthusiasm than he'd shown all lesson. Once perfectly positioned in a spot where the sunlight caught the shimmer of his silvery coat, he let out a sharp whinny and pawed the ground for attention. The riders looked up. Maltie tossed his mane, swished his tail and wheeled his hindquarters around until someone took the bait. Finally the group began to sing:

"Maltie Delight! The bowl to start your day right! Keep trotting from morning to night with the crunchy wholegrain of … Mal-tie Dee-light!"

It was the jingle from Maltie Delight's old advert and exactly what Rose's pony was waiting to hear. With pride he broke into a well-worn routine, stamping his two front feet, nodding his head and letting out another giant whinny. The singers giggled. "He is a funny pony," one of them said, shooting a sidelong glance at Rose.

It had become a daily battle. Rose felt more like

Maltie Delight's minder than his owner as she tried to persuade him to cross the yard. "Come on Maltie, back to your stable now."

Her impression of being perfectly-in-charge fooled no one. Rose tugged on the reins but Maltie dug his heels in. As always, Rose had to wait until her pony felt he had received enough admiring attention. Rose knew this was taking longer than it used to. The novelty of having a celebrity pony at Plum Orchard had begun to wane. People were singing the jingle with less enthusiasm than they once had and taking fewer photos. And every day her pony was showing off more and more outrageously in his desire to be noticed.

A week later matters came to a head. Miss Pickford was in a good mood for once, bellowing "Heels down!" "Wrong leg!" and "SEAT girl!" slightly less than usual during the lesson. As a mark of almost-approval she allowed Rose and Maltie to have an actual canter at the end of the lesson. Only a very short one – they'd barely completed half a circuit before Miss Pickford called, "That's enough of that! Bring him back to a walk and we'll finish with exercises in the saddle."

Rose dutifully attempted to slow Maltie. She heard familiar music coming from outside. Maltie heard it too.

"Maltie Delight! The bowl to start your day right!"

The jingle was booming out of the stable yard radio. The effect on Maltie was electric. Ignoring all Rose's aids, he put his head down and cantered straight out of the school.

"Come back this instant! Have you NO control over your pony at all?" Miss Pickford shouted after Rose. "Next lesson you're returning entirely to sitting trot!"

Maltie skidded to a halt in the yard and stood by the radio quivering and alert. Rose slid off his back. It was his jingle, but now she could hear it had changed. This version had extra drums, and a high-pitched voice broke in to rap in the middle: "Yo breakfast fam this is MD Cheeky. And I'm telling you if you wanna be fleeky, the pengest crunch ain't avocado. Wake up to Malties 'n' reach El Dorado."

"It's the new ad for Maltie Delight. Have you seen it?" Sian Hamill, owner of a solid cob called Rhonda, called over from where she was plaiting her horse's scratchy mane. "Hang on. I'll show you on YouTube..." She waved her mobile phone at Rose. "Can you believe it? After all those years too!"

"Believe what?" asked Rose. It was nice to be spoken to by one of Plum Orchard's proper pony people. Mostly they ignored her and she was too shy to approach them.

Maltie was already pulling across to nose in closer to Sian's phone.

"It's all computer animated. And they're not using a pony any more. Look!"

Rose and Maltie peered at the small screen. "Oh! How strange. Is that..." Rose put her head on one side and squinted at a character with a medallion, "...a rat? In a sombrero?" She listened again to the rap. "It's really terrible."

"I know! 'MD Cheeky'. They've rebranded but I think it's a mistake." Sian looked crestfallen. "I guess that means the end of their 'Win A Pony' competitions. I'll never get a beautiful pony like yours now. You'll be the last ever winner." She scowled and tugged crossly at poor Rhonda's uneven plaits.

Maltie's attention was still fixed on the phone screen. His nostrils quivered and his ears went back. He let out a sharp whinny and backed up, throwing his head up violently. Rose's shoulder was almost yanked out of its socket.

"Maltie! What's wrong? What are you doing?" A sharp flashback of a mint choc chip cornet disappearing into a gaping horse mouth came back to Rose and she flinched. Ponies were unpredictable...

But Maltie dropped his head down. In fact his whole body sagged. He blew out a deep sigh, turned and followed Rose obediently as she led him towards his stable. He suddenly looked less like a magnificent almost-unicorn and more like all the other riding school ponies. He'd seen the future of cereal and he understood: he wasn't included.

"Do you think he's depressed? Can horses get depressed?" Rose asked Carolyn. She was sitting on an upturned bucket in Maltie's stable watching Carolyn brush her pony down with her usual brisk competence. Maltie was pulling mouthfuls from his hay net and chewing them slowly.

"I'm sure they can," said Carolyn. "And I suppose this has been a big change for him. Missing your old showbiz life are you?" Carolyn slapped Maltie's bum affectionately. "He's eating fine; he looks OK to me. Is he not behaving in your lessons?"

"He's perfectly behaved in those," Rose sighed and nibbled her fingernails. "Well, most of the time anyway. I still have no real idea what I'm supposed to be doing."

"Last lesson I saw, you seemed to be coming on

really well. You just need a bit more confidence and some buddies to ride with." Carolyn looked at Rose thoughtfully. "You do his tail today." She chucked a comb at Rose.

"What if I hurt him?" Rose still felt nervous about pony care, especially when it involved getting close to either teeth or back legs.

"I'm sure you'll be gentler than me."

Rose pulled the teeth carefully through the silky silver threads of Maltie's tail. Maltie cocked up one hoof, shifted his weight and farted. Rose paused, then decided to take it as a sign her pony was relaxed. She carried on her tentative combing.

"Maltie's been flat for the last month really; ever since he saw that new advert," Rose explained to Carolyn. "Have you seen the MD Cheeky billboards going up? We saw one on our hack out with Miss Pickford yesterday and Maltie wouldn't trot at all after that. He knows he's been replaced and he thinks I'm a poor substitute for life in a film studio."

"Of course he doesn't! Of course you're not," said Carolyn. "Much nicer for him to have a proper owner who loves him rather than all that celebrity nonsense."

Rose didn't answer. She still didn't feel like a "proper" owner. Much worse and never to be admitted to Carolyn or anyone: did she love Maltie Delight? He didn't seem to be that bothered about her. And having to come to the stables every day to be yelled at by Miss Pickford was not as much of a

fantastic treat as everyone seemed to think it should be.

Carolyn gathered up her brushes to leave. At the stable door she turned back to Rose. "I don't know about Maltie Delight, but I can see you're not quite as happy as you could be Rose. I wonder if a holiday might be a good idea for the two of you."

"A holiday?"

"Didn't your prize include a riding camp? I think it's time you took that up."

"Wouldn't I have to look after Maltie on my own there? I couldn't do that. I might do it all wrong and ruin him! What would Miss Pickford say?"

"Of course you could look after him!" said Carolyn. "And they'd give you plenty of help I'm sure. I'll speak to Miss Pickford. A holiday might be just what you need. What both of you need." Carolyn let herself out of the stable.

Rose put her forehead against Maltie's neck and listened to the steady chomping of his teeth against hay. What was happening to her life? Hadn't she been perfectly happy before?

Sometimes Rose wished she'd never composed

her embarrassing, never-to-be-admitted-to slogan. Sometimes Rose wished she'd never even heard of the Maltie Delight competition.

CHAPTER FOUR

"This must be it, mustn't it Alice?" asked Rose's dad,
pulling the car and borrowed horsebox into a driveway
a month later.

Rose pressed her face to the window and gulped.
This place looked even more intimidating than Plum
Orchard. Behind imposing iron gates Rose could
see a neatly mown field with identical tents pitched
in lines, opposite rows of clean white loose boxes.
Beyond, children on horseback were trotting round
a woodchipped circle. A woman was standing in the
middle with her hands on her hips, assessing them.
Rose already knew they were all going to despise her.

"Miss Brill's Pony Club Boot Camp," Rose's mum
read the sign on the gates. She looked down and

checked the sheaf of papers on her lap. "No, my mistake. That's not the one they've booked Rose on to." Rose breathed a sigh of relief as her mum continued, "There was a bit of confusion with that Davina PR woman actually when I asked about Rose taking up the camp part of her prize. She was a bit short on the phone. She tried to claim Rose wasn't due a holiday at all but I wasn't having that."

"It's a mistake to try to argue with you – a lesson I learned a long time ago. Onwards then!" Rose's dad grinned and carefully turned the car and horsebox round.

Twenty minutes further on, down increasingly twisty country lanes, Rose's mother consulted her map and started squinting out of the window.

"Slow down Dan, it should be coming up on the left any time now."

"Not sure I can go any slower. Pray nothing comes the other way or we could be stuck here for the week," said Rose's dad, gripping the wheel tightly.

"Hang on... Yes! Look, that must be it." Rose's mum pointed to a rusty farm gate, wedged open with a rock. A hand-painted wooden sign hung off it. It read:

"Billy's Boots: Wild West Camp and Big Country Trail", in slightly smudged red letters. Underneath was a pair of brownish blobs which, through half-closed eyes, half resembled a pair of cowboy boots. Rose's dad swung the car onto a rutted track.

"A Wild West camp? Here?" Rose raised her eyebrows. This definitely wasn't Plum Orchard.

"It doesn't look exactly like the brochure Davina sent through," commented Rose's mum doubtfully.

"Are you sure this is the holiday Rose was supposed to win?" asked Rose's dad. He stopped the car in a muddy and overgrown yard outside a small grey cottage. Rose looked all around but there was no woodchipped riding school in sight.

"I'm not sure of anything, but this is certainly the address Davina gave me after I sent her my 'level three' threatening email," said Rose's mum crisply. Rose bit her lip: her mum could be as scary as Miss Pickford sometimes.

As Rose got out of the car, a couple emerged from the back door of the cottage. The man was dressed in a checked shirt, jeans with a big brass buckle, and a large

cowboy hat. He approached them, smiling broadly. The woman was also in jeans. She had thick red hair piled up on top of her head and dramatic black eye make-up. She was less smiley.

"Mr and Mrs Steggles? And Rose? Well howdy! Howdy to you! You found us OK?" said the man. He spoke in a strange half-American, half not-at-all-American drawl. "Where's that big shot celebrity hoss of yours? We can't wait to meet him – let me help you unload your wagon. I'm Billy McCormack. This here's my wife Jolene. We're so honoured you took up our offer to try Billy's Boots out for size. We hope a hoof print of approval from Maltie Delight will make a big difference to our new venture."

Rose's mum frowned. "New venture? I don't quite understand. We thought Rose's prize would be at an established stables. She's still a beginner you see and she used to be very scared of horses and..."

"Mu-um!" Rose hissed, squirming.

"Oh don't you worry about a thing ma'am," said Billy. "We know what we're doing. Your girl's in safe hands. We've got everything under control here, haven't we Jolene?"

Jolene didn't answer.

"The Good For You Breakfast Cereal Company have paid you for this break?" continued Rose's mum. "I don't want my daughter being taken advantage of to endorse some cowboy operation." She glanced at Billy's hat. "So to speak…"

Billy drew himself up. "I can assure you this is a five star camp and your girl will be getting the best that Billy's Boots can offer!"

"I'll be fine Mum." Rose, who had been ready to make her dad drive them all straight back home, suddenly changed her mind. She wasn't sure what Billy's Boots camp was going to be like but she was certain it was not going to be anything like Plum Orchard. She lugged her enormous rucksack out of the boot, dropped it on the ground and went to help unload Maltie Delight. The pony took in his new surroundings. He rolled his eyes uncertainly and pushed his ears back.

"He's a proper looker. Just like he was on the telly," said Billy. He hummed the jingle. Maltie stomped his feet, whinnied and looked happier.

"Come on Alice," said Rose's dad. "Rose has got her phone if there are any problems. Do her good to have an adventure and build up her confidence."

"Eat fruit Rose. And vegetables. And wash. Call us if you're unhappy or for anything at all and..."

"Go! I love you both. I'll see you in a week," said Rose, hugging her parents. Her dad more or less bundled her mum into the car. Waving, they drove away.

"I'll put that in the barrow," said Billy, looking at Rose's rucksack. "It's muddy down the field with all the rain we've been having."

"Should I settle Maltie into his stable now?" asked Rose, nervously running through a mental checklist of everything Carolyn had taught her.

"Stable?" echoed Billy. "Ah, he won't be needing a stable at this time of year. There'll be no stables when we go out on the trail. We'll turn him out with Dolly and the others. There's trees for shelter if it rains. The ponies can get acquainted while you kids do the same."

"I'm not sure he's ever been turned out," said Rose, glancing across at her pony. Jolene was stroking down his nose and whispering to him. Rose was relieved to see Maltie Delight's ears were pricked forwards again. "He's got his own stable at Plum Orchard and before that he lived at the film studio lot."

"He's a hoss. He'll work it out." Billy tipped back his cowboy hat and started pushing the wheelbarrow through the mud. "Follow me. The others are putting up their tents but as a celebrity endorser you'll be in our glamping yurt."

Rose felt her cheeks burn with a familiar red flush. "Are there many other campers?"

Now Billy looked uncomfortable. "No, not too many. Just three for the week including you. Thought it best to keep it simple for the trial run."

"Oh!" said Rose. "So this really is your first camp?"

"It's not a problem," Billy sounded defensive. "Me and Jolene got big plans for Billy's Boots. You and your off-the-telly pony are going to get the full Wild West ranch experience, don't you worry."

"Of course! It's my first camp too. And Maltie Delight's, I think. We're happy with anything. At least I am – Maltie can be fussier," said Rose. "I didn't mean..."

"Here we are then," interrupted Billy. "There's Dolly, see?"

He pushed open a gate and pointed to a shaggy coated cow with impressive horns at the other end of the large field.

There were two ponies grazing near the cow: a big dark bay and a small piebald. The three of them were cropping grass close to where a river ran through the bottom of the field. A short distance away, two figures were busy with sheets of billowing khaki, mallets and poles, putting up small tents.

Along from them, a round tent three times the size and big enough to stand up in had already been pitched. It was a bit grey and patched-up in places but covered with multicoloured bunting and twinkling fairy lights.

"That's your yurt," Billy said proudly. "Got the whole kit second-hand off eBay last week. Me and Jolene got plans to use it for pamper parties and yoga retreats too."

He began to push and squelch the wheelbarrow through the field. The other two children stopped putting up their tents and watched. Rose looked down at her feet, wishing hard that she could be in a normal tent like them.

"Leave your stuff in here then it's time to chow down, sing songs round the campfire and get an early night," said Billy. "We'll start on your ranching skills first thing tomorrow."

"OK," said Rose, pushing open the flap door of the yurt. "Oh!"

Inside the tent was stuffed with a jumble of old rugs, random cushions and throws, a lot more bunting, plastic fruit and flowers, painted glass jam jars and fairy light lanterns. Nothing matched anything else.

"Nice isn't it? Got the idea from a magazine," Billy said proudly.

There was a sharp whinny from outside. Rose stepped out and saw Jolene back at the gate holding Maltie Delight. Silhouetted against the late evening sunshine, the pony looked as glorious as ever. Jolene undid his leading rope and gave an encouraging slap on his rump. Maltie didn't move.

"Maltie!" Rose called, trying to sound commanding. Her pony looked down at her and then, with exaggerated high steps as if he was trying to make a point about the field she was expecting him to live in, picked a path across the grass to a spot as far away from Rose and all the other ponies as he could get.

"Wow! Is that...?"

Rose looked over and saw the two other children had finished putting up their tents and were gazing at Maltie Delight.

"Yes," she said, trying to swallow down her anxiety about talking to new people.

"Seriously? You won the competition?" asked one of them, a boy with glasses.

"Yes," said Rose again, waiting for what would come next.

"No WAY! That's so cool! I entered it too. Everyone I know entered. You actually won?! What was your slogan?"

"I was very lucky," countered Rose, hoping that would be enough.

"Super lucky," agreed the other camper, a girl with a neat black bob. She assessed Maltie with a professional air. "He's certainly got excellent conformation. What's he like to ride?"

"Perfect," said Rose. "Not that I've got any pony to compare him too. I hadn't ridden at all before I won him."

The boy and girl stared at her open-mouthed.

"Seriously?" said the boy. "You are the luckiest lucky person in the whole world. You know that, right?"

"Yes," agreed Rose, trying to pretend that was a very original thing to have heard.

"Right y'all," Billy butted in. "Come on up to the courtyard behind the shower block. There's Jolene's home-made lemonade waiting. I'll get the fire going and dinner on."

"Great, I'm starving," said the boy. "What's for dinner?"

"Proper cowboy food," said Billy.

They looked at him questioningly.

"Beans of course! And plenty of 'em."

CHAPTER FIVE

"You're the flo-wer on my cactus, the shine on my sheriff's staaaar!" Billy sang as he played his guitar. The three children gazed uncomfortably into the charred remains of the campfire and abandoned the last of their beans. There really had been plenty of them.

Rose's fellow campers were called Otto and Mei. Otto's pony was the bay, Dougal, and Pepper was Mei's piebald mare. After exchanging a few facts they'd all retreated into silence. Rose was sure they both thought she was pathetic. Mei seemed to have been riding her entire life and probably had a trophy cabinet of cups and rosettes at home, while Otto lived on a farm. He would be completely at home looking after animals.

Billy and Jolene, on the other hand, didn't seem so certain about what they were doing. The campfire had taken a long time to light. Billy had struggled to get the flame to catch a single log, try as he might with a cigarette lighter and a lot of crumpled newspaper, while Jolene silently glowered at him. After half an hour of failure, Billy had disappeared and come back with a jerry can of petrol. That had got the campfire roaring. Billy now had a lot less eyebrow.

It started to drizzle. It was enough to stop both the fire and Billy's singalong. "Right cowgirls and cowboy. Time for bed. We'll be up early tomorrow for cattle round-up and lasso practice. Y'all got your torches to find your way down the field?"

Otto and Mei went on ahead. To avoid having to cross the mud twice, Rose visited the toilet and brushed her teeth in the shower block before heading back down to her tent. She whistled as she flicked on her head torch and opened the gate to the field. Six months ago she'd entered a competition on a cereal box, and now she was camping with her very own pony. Maybe she could do adventures. Maybe she could manage a pony on her own for a week.

Rose cast her beam of light around the field and tried to pick out Maltie. The torch caught Otto adjusting Dougal's rug and Mei filling a hay net. A little further on Dolly the cow was grazing, unbothered by the rain that was coming down harder now. So where was Maltie Delight?

Rose swung her head this way and that, trying to take in the whole field. She felt panic rise. She checked again more slowly. And a third time. There was no doubt: Maltie Delight had gone.

Rose raced down the field, slipping and sliding through patches of mud and worse.

"What are you doing?" asked Mei. "Slow down! You're frightening Pepper! Don't you know anything about approaching ponies?"

"Sorry! Help! Please! Have you seen Maltie Delight? I've lost him!"

"He must be around," said Otto. "It's just the dark. Took me a minute to find Dougal."

"Maltie's so pale he glows in the dark!"

"But he can't have got out. The gate was closed and bolted when we came back and we'd have heard him if he'd been in the yard."

"Maybe he's been horsenapped!" cried Rose.

"Could have got into trouble over that way," said Mei, shining her torch towards the hedgerow and river bank beyond the tents. "Horses do slip."

Rose gasped in horror as Mei's shaft of light bounced off fast-flowing water. "I've drowned him! I've been in charge of him for four hours and I've drowned him! I knew he wasn't used to being turned out!"

"You haven't drowned him," said Otto. "That water's not even a metre deep Mei. Maltie's got to be here somewhere. It's a big field. He's probably lying down in a hollow. Let me finish up with Dougal and I'll help you look. Have you got pony nuts on you, or something that he might come for?"

"No..." said Rose, wondering what kind of tree
pony nuts grew on. She thought about Maltie. "He
whinnies when people sing!" she remembered.

"Worth a try," said Otto.

"Maltie Delight! The bowl to start your day right,"
Rose warbled as she stumbled around the sodden
field, listening out for an answering call. "Keep
trotting from morning to night with the crunchy
wholegrain of— oh help, my boot's stuck."

The fairy lights were glowing around her yurt.
As Rose retrieved her boot they started to shake
mysteriously. It was as if they'd been set in motion
by something inside the tent. Something or someone
stamping their hooves…

Rose ran and threw open the flap. "I've found
him!" she called back to Otto and Mei.

Denied a proper stable, Maltie Delight had made
himself completely at home in the only alternative.
He was occupying the yurt as if it had been meant
for him, reclining against a pile of cushions, Rose's
rucksack kicked to one side. The pony turned his

head as Rose entered and stared at her as if she was interrupting him in his private boudoir.

"I haven't killed you! Thank goodness," said Rose. She went to give Maltie a tentative hug but he flinched away from her, twitching as if he'd been bitten. "Oh, I am a bit wet – is that a problem?" said Rose, realising both her hair and coat were dripping. She took off her cagoule and the pony deigned to let her stroke his back.

The noise of rain pattering against the canvas increased. Rose sighed. "I'm not going to persuade you that you belong back outside in that, am I? I'll go and get your hay net."

She put her wet coat back on and squelched off into the dark once more. The hay net was tied to the fence right on the other side of the field. After a lot of fiddling with the wet knot Rose managed to free it. She slung it over one shoulder and started the slippery trudge back towards her yurt. She could see the dark shapes of Dougal and Pepper both grazing peacefully. Otto's and Mei's tents glowed from within, their occupants snuggled dry inside. Why was she out getting soaked?

A few metres away from the yurt's entrance, Rose heard her mobile ringing inside. She ran to answer it and squelched straight into one of Dolly's pats. Her foot skidded out from under her and she tumbled forwards and slid head-first along the wet grass into the tent, plastering her entire front half with mud and worse. Just missing cannoning into Maltie's dry, sparkling white side, Rose threw the soggy hay net at him. "There you go!"

She grabbed her phone.

"Hello? Hello? Rose?" It was her mum.

"How's it going? Missing us yet?" And dad.

"Hi!" said Rose, catching her breath. She tried to sound cheerful. "I'm fine. I'm fine! Everything's totally fine here."

"Are you sure?" Mum again. "You sound funny. You are warm enough and keeping dry, aren't you? Your sleeping bag is supposed to be good to minus thirty degrees; it's the sort they recommend for climbing Everest but it did feel thin to me and—"

"Leave her alone Alice! We agreed, remember? No fussing."

"Sorry," said her mum. "The house feels empty without you Rose! How's looking after Maltie Delight going?"

"So far so good. Maltie is settling in," said Rose, looking across to her pony. To demonstrate just how settled he was feeling, Maltie pushed to his feet, farted loudly and stretched to pull a mouthful from the hay net, grinding his teeth right by the phone.

"What's that noise?" asked her mum. "Some sort of farm machinery? DON'T STICK YOUR ARM IN A THRESHER ROSE! I don't trust the countryside. It's full of danger."

"Mum!" said Rose. "Everything's fine, promise. I'll ring you tomorrow…"

"But you haven't told us—"

"Love you. Bye!"

Rose hung up. She looked around the tent. Given how spacious it had seemed earlier it was now surprisingly full of pony. Rose picked up her sleeping bag. It was heavy and ominously soggy.

"Ew! Maltie! Couldn't you have weed outside? I thought you had perfect manners!"

Maltie lifted his tail, farted again and carried on eating.

"If only your fans could see you now," said Rose. "I can't share a tent with you. One of us has got to go." Maltie paid no attention. "It's going to be me is it?"

Oh yes, that's right, I remember: I am the luckiest lucky person that ever lived, thought Rose, as she curled up on the tack room floor, wrapped in two old horse blankets. She closed her eyes and wondered when sleep would come.

CHAPTER SIX

"Argggggh!"

Mei's scream was a very effective alarm clock. Rose pushed herself off the floor, rubbing her eyes.

Mei put her hand to her chest. "Oh! I thought you were dead!"

"Not dead," confirmed Rose.

"What are you doing in here? Billy called us for breakfast. We need to catch and groom the ponies as well." Mei picked up a tray of brushes. "You're very muddy," she observed. "Did you sleep here?"

"Not much," said Rose, getting to her feet and trying to brush herself down a bit. The tack room floor had been cold, which had at least set the mud on her clothes hard. It flaked off her coat in chunks.

"What are we doing this morning?"

"Billy said something about round up." Mei smiled. "I can't wait until we go out on the trail ride. That's what I came for. I wanted to go to a dude ranch near the Grand Canyon but that was too expensive. One day..."

Rose rubbed the sleep out of her eyes and followed Mei into the sunlight.

"Mornin' campers," said Billy cheerfully. He was stirring a bubbling vat over a gas camping stove in the courtyard; a quicker option than his campfire. "Ready for breakfast? Plenty here."

Rose looked into the pot. More baked beans. "I'd better have a shower and sort out Maltie first," she said politely. She took three slices of bread and jam from a pile on the camp table instead.

It was a beautiful morning. The rain had stopped in the night. When Rose returned to the field she saw the sunshine had even brought Maltie Delight outside. Following his night in tented luxury he appeared refreshed – positively sparkling. He stood on the glistening grass in the top corner of the field with his head turned into the breeze so that his mane fluttered free. He looked like he might be practising a photo-shoot for a new breakfast bar range. Rose smiled; she had to admit he was the best-looking pony.

Otto and Mei were already busy brushing their ponies down. Grooming and tacking up were tasks that Rose had done before, with Carolyn's help. Catching Maltie to start grooming and tacking him up was quite another thing though. At Plum Orchard he'd always been in his stable. Too late Rose realised she should have got Carolyn to talk her through the basics.

Maltie didn't shy or run away when Rose approached. He appeared prepared to cooperate. But just as Rose held out his head collar he shimmied away the precise distance needed to remain out of reach.

She tried again – and again was left empty-handed. Maltie shot Rose a cheeky look from under his forelock.

"Stop grinning at me and stay still!" pleaded

Rose, as Maltie gave her the slip for the tenth time.

"Have you never done this before?" asked Mei, perched on the fence rail and looking impatient. Both Pepper and Dougal were now clean and tacked up.

"No," admitted Rose.

"You need a treat. Something that he wants," advised Otto.

Rose thought for a moment. She reached into her pocket and got out her phone.

"Here Maltie... Want to take a selfie?" she asked, tilting the camera so that the pony's head was caught with hers on the screen.

Maltie turned. His ears pricked as he noticed the camera. And then he came over.

"Gotcha." Rose slipped his head collar on and snapped a picture of them both at the same time.

"Nailed it!"

"Unusual technique," said Otto, nodding. "But effective."

"Lucky," said Mei.

"He's shameless," said Rose. She smiled and patted Maltie's neck proudly.

Everybody groomed, dressed, tacked up and fed, Rose, Otto and Mei mounted their ponies and waited by the gate of the large meadow on the other side of the farm cottage. Jolene was watching them through the window, but when Rose waved at her she twitched the curtain shut.

"I'm not sure Jolene signed up to Billy's Boots camp," said Rose.

"She's supposed to be teaching us line dancing and rhinestone craft this week," said Mei. "Maybe she's just not into riding."

"Ah," said Rose, feeling shifty; maybe she and Jolene had something in common.

Near a large pond in the far corner of the meadow Billy was laying out traffic cones, a plastic tunnel and a large wooden A-frame ramp. The last didn't look like it would take a pony's weight. Rose wondered nervously if they were going to be told to jump them or do rodeo stunts. Billy walked over to them.

"Howdy!" he said. "Ready for round-up? Planning to buy in Western-trained hosses and a whole herd of ranch cattle, but right now we're working with what we've got. Any of your ponies trained to neck rein?"

Rose, Otto and Mei looked blank. Billy looked disappointed.

"Never mind, I thought as much. Whatever style you ride, you can still ranch."

"Where are the cattle?" asked Otto.

Billy ran a finger around his shirt collar and didn't meet Otto's eye. "We-eell... Guess you've met Dolly already."

"Is Dolly all you've got?" said Otto.

"Oh, I've got more livestock..." Billy went over to two large wicker crates and opened the lids.

Six white ducks popped their heads out and stretched their wings. They took one look at the ponies and flapped and waddled away down the meadow as fast as they could.

"Duck herding!" said Mei. "Seriously?"

Billy grinned. "Get them all round the cones, over the ramp, through the tunnel, past the pond and into the corral over there, see? Off you go."

Billy took himself off to sit on the fence and watch.

"OK, easy-peasy." Mei kicked Pepper into action. They cantered after the ducks. But as soon as the pony came close the ducks fluffed up in outrage and scattered all over the meadow.

"OK, impossible!" called Mei after charging up and down for several minutes.

"You're scaring them," said Otto. "We should cover their escape routes and be stealthy. Come back at a walk along the right-hand side. Rose, cut them off before the pond. Me and Dougal will take it slowly from behind. Dougal's good at slow."

They stuck in formation, changing rein, circling and turning whenever a duck tried to break away. Rose felt less self-conscious about her riding having a task to focus on. The birds finally came together into a single group and were persuaded to waddle around the first cone.

"Yes!" said Mei, punching the air.

Rose urged Maltie forwards to block a gap as the ducks veered to the other side. They successfully turned the ducks back and round the other cones. Eventually the ducks clustered at the bottom of the ramp.

"Come in tight on either side of me now," said Otto to Rose and Mei. He made encouraging clucky-quacks under his tongue as the first duck put a webbed foot on the ramp. "That's it, you can do it," he coaxed.

The ducks padded obediently up and down the ramp then through the tunnel in single file.

"What are you – some kind of weird duck whisperer?" asked Mei.

As the ducks emerged from the tunnel one veered off from the pack.

"She wants to go swimming! We'll lose her," warned Otto. "Quick Rose!"

Rose tried to turn Maltie to head off the escapee at the muddy edge of the pond, but this time her pony was resistant. As soon as his hooves touched the sludgier ground he threw his head up and backed away with an outraged whinny. Rose lost her stirrups and had to grab on to Maltie's mane to stay on. She was getting the impression that she had more of a city pony. Maltie knew how to deal with the paparazzi, but ponds were a new experience.

It didn't matter; his whinny was enough to startle the wayward duck and send her waddling back to the safety of the pack.

"Well done Maltie!" said Otto.

They edged the ducks towards the final corral and held their breath as one by one the birds padded inside. Otto shut the gate and the three duck ranchers high-fived each other. They felt like they'd brought a whole herd of cattle down from a mountain valley.

Billy walked over and tipped his hat back. "Good job," he said.

"It was mostly down to you Otto," Rose said. "I guess you've been moving animals around all your life."

Otto looked surprised. "I haven't," he said.

"I thought you lived on a farm?"

"My dad works on a farm and we live on the estate. But it's crops: sugar beet and wheat. They don't need herding," said Otto. "It's my hours of teamwork on my Playstation." He grinned. "It's like I tell my mum: it's all about transferable skills."

As they headed back to the courtyard for lunch,

Rose realised that it had been her and Maltie's first ride together where they were making the decisions themselves. With the exception of a few hiccups, it had worked out. Maybe she had learned a little bit about how to ride after all.

CHAPTER SEVEN

Duck herding had broken the ice. Once their ponies had been untacked and turned out to graze, the three ranchers sat on logs in the courtyard and ate hotdogs – hotdogs with beans.

"All my brothers learned to ride on Dougal before me. I'm the fourth to look after him," explained Otto through a mouthful of sausage. "He's one of the family. He lives out in the field by our cottage. I hack him out around the fields when the house gets crowded and my mum chucks me out for fresh air. My brothers still live at home so it's always crowded," Otto added. "My parents were happy to send me away for a bit. Sam will be taking over my half of our bedroom with the tractor engine he's stripping."

"Your family sound great," said Rose. She tried to imagine what it might be like to have three big brothers instead of it just being her at home.

"They're terrible," said Otto. "My family forget I even exist. Last week nobody bothered to tell me lunch was ready and by the time I got to the table there were no roast potatoes left."

"Don't worry. We'll always save you some beans," said Mei.

"Plenty of beans," agreed Rose.

"Anyone want more beans?" asked Billy, appearing from the cottage just at that moment. They stifled giggles.

"What are we doing this afternoon Billy?" asked Rose.

"If you've finished, wash your plates and come down to the bottom of the garden. I'm going to teach you how to rope a cow."

The cow was already waiting for them when they got there. It looked a lot like a bale of straw. It had a cabbage for a head and two dried corncobs skewered on for horns.

"Easier to start with than Dolly. Don't reckon she'd fancy being lassoed much," explained Billy. "Take a rope each and I'll show you how to make coils."

Each of the ropes had a little loop at one end. "That's called the honda," said Billy. "Post the other end through it to make a big circle and keep the rest of the rope flat and straight in coils in your other hand." Rose and the others tried to follow his instructions. "That's it… Now you swing that big loop round nice and easy at shoulder height – just like this, see... And when you're ready you release it so that— Oh!"

Billy released his rope but it didn't snag either of the corncob horns. Instead it flew in the opposite direction, caught on the washing line and pulled it and all the freshly laundered whites down to the ground.

A yell came from the cottage. "BILLY!"

"Yes. Well. You get the idea," said Billy. "Um … have a practice and I'll come and see how you're getting on in a while."

He tipped his hat forwards, gathered up the dirty clothes and slunk off to placate Jolene.

"Do you think Billy knows anything about cattle roping?" asked Mei. She was already circling her lasso around her head. She released the loop. It went exactly where it was supposed to, catching on to one of the corncobs. Mei put her hands on her hips in satisfaction.

"Wow!" Otto had a go, but his loop somehow got smaller as he circled it and then collapsed. "I'm doing something wrong. I did see Billy watching a guide to rope skills on his phone over lunch – maybe we should look at that."

Billy didn't return. There were raised voices from the cottage. Rose, Otto and Mei carried on coiling in and throwing out their ropes. Only Mei had the hang of it. She caught the straw bale every time.

"It's like hula-hooping," she advised. "You need to move your whole arm and upper body."

"That's no help, I can't hula-hoop either," said Rose, gazing at her rope lying limply on the ground.

"Hey look – I can lasso myself!" Otto was tied up in his own knot. "But can I get out again?" He fought with the coils of rope around his middle.

Rose took pity and helped him free. "I don't think you should become an escapologist," she said.

"Let's stop this and have a ride. We could hack out on the bridleway along the river," suggested Mei.

"Do you think we're allowed?" asked Rose.

She'd never hacked Maltie out anywhere other than short trips trailing behind Miss Pickford down the road by Plum Orchard.

"I'll knock on the cottage door and let Billy know," said Mei. "We don't need to go far."

Billy nodded and waved at them vaguely when Mei asked. Jolene was still yelling in the background. "Sure, go exploring," he said. "Camp dinner at six. Cowboy stew on the menu tonight!"

They saddled up and walked the ponies past the

tents and through the gate at the bottom of the field, following a path with a bridleway symbol along the river. Willow leaves trailed in the water, making a maze where paddling moorhens played peek-a-boo. The hedgerow on the other side of the path was full of flowers and humming with bees and butterflies. It was a gorgeous afternoon. Rose turned her face up to the sky and breathed deeply. Maltie's walk underneath her felt loose and free. Rose relaxed her shoulders. She had to admit, this really was … nice.

If only riding was always as easy as this.

"Pepper's longing to stretch her legs," called Mei from the front. "We're going to canter now. Who's coming?"

She didn't wait for a reply; kicking forwards, she and Pepper raced away down the path.

"How about it Dougal?" asked Otto, shortening his reins. "Just a short one, I promise."

After quite a lot of encouragement, the big bay lumbered into a bouncy trot, which eventually became a slow, sure-footed canter. With steadiness rather than style the pair disappeared after Pepper and Mei.

Maltie's ears pricked up. He lifted his head and started to sidle and jog. Rose's stomach lurched: could she do this too? It was strange not to have Miss Pickford to give her permission. Rose tightened her reins, gently squeezed Maltie's sides and they set off after the others.

Cantering through open countryside was much, much better than being in the arena at Plum Orchard. Hedgerow, field and river streaked past in a blur of green and blue. Maltie's canter was smooth as whipped cream. Rose felt connected with her pony in a way she'd not experienced before: like they were one thing rather than two. She felt bigger, stronger, more special. Maltie's head arched forwards, and his beautiful silver mane streamed up and out to one side like a waterfall. They were in perfect harmony. He was her pony. Hers!

"Ohhhhhh!" sighed Rose, a smile plastered across her pink-cheeked and tingling face. This was quickly followed by "OH!" as Maltie screeched to a shuddering halt.

Rose kept moving. She slid off Maltie's perfect

back and onto the ground with a splash and a thump. "Ow! EW!"

"Ah…" said Mei. "Didn't you see that coming?"

Maltie Delight had stopped dead before getting so much as one pristine hoof in the deep muddy puddle that Rose now found herself in, soaked through and filthy from top to toe.

Rose looked down at herself ruefully. She was going to have a whole lot of new bruises to add to her collection.

"I don't think Maltie likes getting his hooves dirty. Celebrities, eh?" said Otto, swallowing down laughter. He and Mei and their ponies were a little freckled with dirt where they'd slowed and trotted through the puddle, but Rose's mud-out was a total festival of splatter.

"No," said Rose, narrowing her eyes and staring at her unrepentant pony. "He really doesn't." And you really are a useless rider, the voice inside her head added. Rose felt tears bubbling and gave a big sniff.

Mei turned Pepper and looked away tactfully. "Pepper doesn't mind mud but she's not good with loud noises. I've fallen before when she's been startled."

"It's flapping plastic things for Dougal," said Otto. "Tricky when they've wrapped the bales in it at harvest time. Broke my collarbone once. Time we were all heading back anyway."

Rose didn't really believe Mei and Otto had ever fallen off but she was grateful for their kindness. Getting her tears under control, she wiped her face without thinking and smeared mud across the one part of her that had been clean. She suddenly wished she could be magicked back to her room at home to hide under her duvet. All it would take was a phone call and her parents would come and this could all be over.

Rose straightened her back. "Come on Maltie." She turned her pony around and put her foot in the stirrup to remount. Maltie took one look at her dripping, filthy state and wheeled his hindquarters away.

"MALTIE!" said Rose, hopping about. "Stop moving!"

She held his head more firmly and took hold of the stirrup again. Maltie put his ears back and swished his tail angrily but this time Rose managed to swing herself into the saddle.

Silently and sulkily, they followed the others back down the bridleway towards the camp. Maltie's back was hunched and his ears flattened for the entire way. He gave an extravagant, twitching shiver of disgust every time Rose's legs made contact with his sides.

Rose watched the mud trickle down her legs, where it dried in the sun. She looked like a squashed chocolate bar, but she didn't smell like one. Maltie obviously hated her; she would never ever cut it as a rider. She was a hopeless human being.

CHAPTER EIGHT

Pink, scrubbed and shivering, Rose emerged from the shower. Her phone was ringing in her bag.

"Hi sweetpea, it's us! How are you? Have you had a wonderful day?"

"Hi Mum, hi Dad." Rose felt a wave of homesickness at hearing their voices.

"What have you been up to? Tell us everything."

"I've been herding and lassoing and we went for a ride out." Rose decided to tell them some things.

"Sounds fun! Are you making friends with the other campers?" asked Rose's dad.

"Yes." This at least was the truth. "They're good riders but not show-offs about it. They're helping me."

"I hope Billy is supervising you all carefully," said

Rose's mum.

"He's cooking us lots of vegetables. We get plenty with every meal. And I'm keeping very clean. I've just had my second shower of the day, in fact."

"Good!" said Rose's dad. "That's excellent news Rosie. We'll call again tomorrow."

"But I haven't asked her anything yet..." Rose's mum interrupted.

"She's still alive. We don't need any more than that."

Rose listened to her mum and dad arguing and smiled. "Bye! Love you," she cut in.

Her dad was right; she was still alive. And now she no longer looked like a mud monster she felt happier – although she wasn't looking forward to the next job. Rose picked up her pile of dirty clothes and stinking sleeping bag, walked across the courtyard and knocked on the cottage door.

Jolene answered. She was talking on the phone. "Stop tempting me Bobby. I promised those days were over..." She covered the receiver. "Yes?" she asked Rose.

Rose looked at her feet. "I'm sorry to bother you but

I was wondering if I could maybe use your washing machine? I got really muddy out riding today and I don't think I can wear these things again. There was also a bit of an accident with my sleeping bag..." Rose went red. "Not that sort of accident – well, yes, sort of that sort of accident, but not me – my pony! It really wasn't me..." she babbled.

To her surprise Jolene's face softened."These things happen. Help yourself. It's through there. Washing powder is on the side."

Still scarlet, Rose ducked under Jolene's arm and into the stone-floored kitchen. She'd never used a washing machine before but there was no way she was going to ask Jolene for any more help. Bundling everything into the machine, Rose shook in powder on top, selected the first program on the dial and hoped for the best. The machine rumbled into life.

Rose looked around. The kitchen was small and crowded with pictures and knick-knacks. She took in the stack of jumbo-sized cans of baked beans lined up against one wall. Some of them were the kind that had little sausages and potatoes in; that was tonight's cowboy stew, Rose guessed.

The walls were hung with photos of American scenes: real-life cowboys and cowgirls bull-riding at rodeos and galloping across cactus-peppered deserts. There was a framed sheriff's badge, a bandana and a tin sign saying Route 66. On the ledge over the fireplace were more photographs and a giant framed gold record. Rose went over to have a closer look. The photos were of a band. The red-haired lead singer, dressed in a leather mini skirt and smiling and waving at a cheering crowd, looked familiar. The plaque underneath the record read "Presented to Jo-Jo and the Mustang Boys to commemorate their Number One selling album."

"It was a long time ago."

Rose spun around. Jolene was standing in the doorway watching her.

"You're Jo-Jo!" said Rose, suddenly connecting the confident woman singing in the photo with the less smiley version in front of her now.

"Was," corrected Jolene. "And Billy was a Mustang Boy. But not any more." She sighed. "You can go.

I'll put your things on to dry when
they're done and bring them out to you."
She indicated the door with her head. Rose
scurried out.

In the field Mei was practising handstands and
Otto was reading on the grass. Dougal and Pepper
were grazing but Maltie Delight was standing to one
side. He snorted when he saw Rose and trotted up to
her, sniffing at her curiously.

Mei dropped down from her handstand. "Look –
he's come to say sorry for dumping you in mud soup."

"Probably likes the smell of my apple shower gel,"
said Rose. "Don't think I've forgiven you," she added
to Maltie, but she stroked his silky neck.

"He is a funny pony," said Mei. "He doesn't seem used to being in a field."

"That's because he's not," said Rose. "I think he's been kept stabled pretty much for ever."

"Oh that's so sad!" said Otto. "He needs reminding how being outside works. Come on Maltie; this is called grass. Try it. You'll love it." He picked a handful and held it out to the pony. "It's like hay, only greener and wetter. Mmmmm!"

Rose giggled. She got onto her hands and knees and mimed eating. "Oh yes I looooove grass. Grass is delicious!"

"Save some for me!" said Mei, picking handfuls and throwing them in the air.

They were all laughing now.

Maltie looked down his nose at them

as if he thought they were behaving very immaturely and wandered off towards his yurt.

"Did you know Jolene used to be a singer in a band with Billy?" said Rose once they had stopped giggling. "Quite a big one I think. I saw photos in the cottage."

"Bit different from running a riding camp," said Mei. "Must be why she's grumpy now. Imagine having been a star playing in front of crowds and then finding yourself heating up beans with Billy."

"Maybe she loves Billy," said Otto. Rose and Mei both looked at him with disgust. "What?"

"I reckon Jolene feels the same way about ending up with Billy as Maltie does about ending up with me," said Rose with a sigh.

That night Rose felt more bone-tired than ever before in her life; her eyelids were drooping like in a cartoon. It was just as well that bedtime was called early after a whittling demonstration by Billy was cut short. Going the wrong way with his knife like he had with his lasso, Billy whittled his own thumb. He had to use his bandana to soak up all the blood.

When she reached the yurt Rose was relieved to find it was unoccupied. Her clean sleeping bag had been laid out inside. The night was clear and Maltie Delight was at the other end of the field, the light from the full moon making his coat shine extra sparkly. Rose was sure her pony knew exactly the magical picture he was presenting.

Around three in the morning Rose came round from a strange dream about lassoing cans of beans and chasing ducks made of mud, woken by a rustling noise. She half opened her eyes and drew in breath, suddenly more awake. The door flap of the yurt was wide open. A grey face was poking through the canvas, staring at Rose. For an unnerving moment she thought she was being haunted by a horse-shaped ghost. She blinked hard and two other faces appeared: one bay and one piebald. It was Maltie – and it seemed he had been making friends.

Rose sat up. "I'm pleased you're all getting along but it's not the time to invite everyone round to our place. This isn't a night club or a 24-hour garage. It isn't a stable either. Go away! Go and eat grass like normal ponies." She slumped down and burrowed back inside her sleeping bag.

"Moooooo!"

Rose sat up again and saw a horned head had joined the other three. Four pairs of nostrils snorted and blew in clouds of steam.

"What do you all want?" Rose rummaged around in her rucksack. She found a packet of energy bars that her mum had packed for emergencies. "If you have these what am I going to eat when I can't face beans?"

Breaking the bars in half, she held out a piece flat on her hand to each of the animals in turn and tried not to think about the ice-cream cornet incident.

There were a lot of ticklish whiskers and soft lips and slurpy tongues, but no gnashing teeth.

Rose wiped the drool on her sleeping bag. "Back to the field!" she directed.

One by one, the horned, piebald and bay heads disappeared. Maltie lingered a while longer, watching Rose. Finally, he lowered his head just outside the yurt and took a mouthful of grass. He chewed it with a slightly uncertain expression before going for another.

"See? We told you you'd like it," said Rose. She snuggled back down in her warm sleeping bag and shut her eyes. She could hear Maltie cropping and grinding blades of grass. Occasionally he snorted in a satisfied way and swished his tail against the canvas of the yurt. They were good sounds to fall asleep to.

CHAPTER NINE

"Are you sure this is allowed Billy?" asked Mei the next day. "Only I've never heard of anyone taking a cow for a walk before."

They were attempting to ride out along the same bridleway they'd followed yesterday, this time in the opposite direction. Billy and Dolly were with them.

"Course it's allowed!" said Billy. "What do you think being a cowhand is all about? You've got to move your livestock. Those ducks yesterday were just the beginning. Now we're scaling up."

"We might get further if you were on a horse too," said Rose, but she said it quietly. It felt a bit mean to pick holes. Billy already had his hands full, and one of them was in a bandage after his whittling accident. He had Dolly on a halter and was attempting to lead her along like a dog. Dolly didn't seem sold on the idea. Or at least not on the moving part of it – she was happy to be out of the field. As soon as Billy had opened the gate, she'd charged straight out to a particularly lush patch of long green grass. Then she'd put her head down to graze and hadn't looked up since, no matter how much Billy pulled on her rope.

"She must have had her eye on that grass for weeks," said Otto. "It's always greener..."

"Come on! Me and Pepper are bored," said Mei, wheeling round in circles on her pony.

Rose could feel Maltie was full of fresh-air energy too. He bounced and snatched at his bit in an excitable mood. Rose stroked his neck. She wondered nervously how many deep puddles were on the bridleway in this direction.

"Come on Dolly," said Billy, hauling on the halter again. "We'll never make it to the weir for lunch at this rate."

Dolly ignored him.

"Maybe she'll follow us if we go on ahead?"

suggested Mei, looking down the path longingly. "She'll want to stay with her herd."

"Or maybe we should try to push her on from behind like we did with the ducks," countered Otto.

A jangling chorus of bells interrupted their deliberations. Twenty-five cyclists suddenly came speeding round the corner. All the riders and ponies were startled by the sea of brightly coloured Lycra but none of them more than Dolly. The cow now moved fast. Billy, holding on to her rope, moved with her.

"Ahhhhh! Stop! Dolly... STOP!" shouted Billy.

Rose, Mei and Otto watched in horror as Billy was pulled off his feet. His hat went flying. As the cyclists scattered and tumbled out of the way, Billy was dragged along the ground behind the charging cow.

"Let go of the rope Billy! LET GO!" shouted Otto.

"Dooolllllyyyyyy!" Billy shouted one last time as he finally let go. He rolled onto his back, looking stunned, and the cow raced out of sight.

"We've got ourselves a round up!" said Mei, pointing at the cloud of dust left by Dolly. "I'm going after her. Yee-ha!" She kicked Pepper and the two of them raced

away down the path.

The cyclists picked themselves and their bicycles
up. One of them stuck out a hand and helped Billy
to his feet. After they had both brushed themselves
down, they began shouting at each other. Rose and
Otto politely pretended not to listen.

"Are you OK Billy?" checked Rose. She could
feel Maltie bounce and jog on the spot, eager to
follow Pepper.

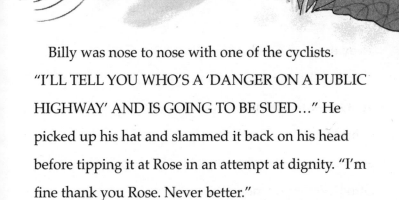

Billy was nose to nose with one of the cyclists.
"I'LL TELL YOU WHO'S A 'DANGER ON A PUBLIC
HIGHWAY' AND IS GOING TO BE SUED…" He
picked up his hat and slammed it back on his head
before tipping it at Rose in an attempt at dignity. "I'm
fine thank you Rose. Never better."

"We'll go after Dolly then," said Otto.

"Go ahead," said Billy, rolling up his sleeves.
"I'll come and find you as soon as I've dealt with

these LIVESTOCK-FRIGHTENING CLOWNS ON WHEELS."

As she urged Maltie into a canter, Rose tried to concentrate and not get completely carried away this time. She imagined a tiny Miss Pickford on her shoulder yelling instructions in her ear. "Heels DOWN I said! Keep contact! LOOK where you are going!"

When Maltie swerved off the dirt track and onto fresh grass Rose stayed with him and even managed to keep her stirrups. Up ahead she could see Mei, Pepper, Otto and Dougal had stopped. Rose sat back and tightened her grip on the reins and Maltie slowed in response.

"I think I've found Dolly," said Mei, pointing.

"Ah," said Rose, seeing the problem.

"Oh no," said Otto. "Is she stuck?"

At a sharp bend in the bridleway Dolly had charged straight on. Only her back end was visible, sticking out of a thick bramble hedge. Her front half was poking through the other side. A low and pitiful "MOOOOOOOOOO" and violent shaking of the leaves confirmed she was wedged tight.

"How are we going to get her out?" asked Rose.

"I could lasso her and we could pull her out if we had rope," said Mei confidently. Otto and Rose exchanged sceptical glances.

"We don't have rope," said Otto.

"Should we just wait for Billy?" suggested Rose.

"Like Billy's going to know what to do! Come on Pepper." Mei was already exploring along the hedge. "There's a low point here and the landing looks clear. I'm going to jump over."

She turned her pony and urged her into a canter once more. They flew over the hedge. "Dolly's horns are tangled in brambles," Mei called from the other side. "I can try to free them but it's going to be tricky."

"Be careful Mei. Those horns are pointy," called back Rose.

"I'll come and help," said Otto, lining up Dougal for the jump. "How about you Rose?"

Rose shook her head. "I haven't done much

jumping. Only trotting poles and cavaletti."

"OK, see you in a minute," said Otto. He set Dougal at the hedge and his pony scrambled over.

Rose waited on Maltie, feeling like a spare part. She could hear Otto and Mei snapping branches and making soothing noises to the cow.

"That's it, almost enough room. She might back out suddenly Rose, so give her some space," called Otto.

A boy on a BMX came round the corner of the bridleway. At the sight of Maltie he screeched on his brakes. His mouth gaped. "Is that...?"

"Yes," said Rose, twisting to try to keep an eye on Dolly who was thrashing around in the hedge. The boy got out his phone to take a picture and Maltie began posing for his new fan.

"Did you win...?"

"Yeah."

"Not fair, I entered that! You're the luckiest…"

"Yup."

"What was your slogan then?"

Rose finally turned her attention away from Dolly's bottom. "Um... I..."

"SHE'S FREE!" yelled Otto. "GET OUT OF THE WAY ROSE!"

Dolly plunged backwards out of the hedge. She celebrated freedom in the best way she knew: by lifting her tail and letting rip a spray of fresh, green-brown cowpat. Rose and Maltie, facing the wrong way at the wrong time, were caught full on by the spray. They were pebble-dashed from their ears to their feet.

Maltie let out his most horrified whinny yet. From a standing start he jumped over the back wheel of the boy's bicycle, put his head down and hurtled back

down the track. Rose clung on for her first ever full-throttle gallop.

Billy, wandering idly up the path in search of his campers, only just had time to scramble to one side as the dripping brown Rose and Maltie streaked past him. They thundered all the way back to the farm.

CHAPTER TEN

"At least you stayed on," said Otto. "That was really impressive under the circumstances."

"And I saw Maltie jumped that bike very cleanly," said Mei. "See how easy it is? You didn't need to be scared. It looked like a great gallop. I'd have enjoyed it."

"Even covered in cowpat?" asked Rose, towelling her hair dry after yet another quick shower and change. "All right Maltie, I'm coming!"

In the field Maltie was neighing in outrage, waiting for Rose to come and give him his own wash.

"He looks like a Dalmatian pony with all those spots on his white coat," said Otto. "He's turned into an Appaloosa."

"He doesn't want spots though," said Rose as Maltie

made another screeching whinny.
"Help – I've groomed him but I've
never washed him."

"It's not hard," said Mei. "Have
you got any horse shampoo?"

"No."

"Doesn't really matter; you can use
the human sort. I've done it lots of times.
I'll get a bottle from the shower."

Rose fetched Maltie into the yard, tied him up
and started running the hose. The water was icy
cold. As soon as Rose sprayed him, Maltie flattened
his ears and bared his teeth at her. He was in a
stinking mood as well as stinking.

Rose sighed. "OK, I'll find warmer water, you
prima donna."

She filled a bucket from the hot tap, then started
sponging down Maltie's coat with her wash cloth. His
ears pricked forward again and he put his teeth away.
He kept turning his head to check what Rose was
doing, but made no other objection.

"Honestly – should we play music and light a

scented candle for him too?" said Mei, coming out of the shower block with a large bottle. "I found this. It says it's all natural, it should be fine."

Rose squirted the shampoo over Maltie and began to rub it in. It lathered up beautifully. Now Maltie relaxed. As Rose scrubbed at the patches of poo, he lowered his eyelids and drooped his head as if he were having a massage at a spa.

"I should have given him cucumber slices for his eyes!" Rose laughed as her fingers worked the shampoo around Maltie's ears and into his mane. "Odd that it's lathering up all red though. What's it got in it ... Mei?"

Rose stopped rubbing the shampoo in. Mei had gone rather

pale as she read the side of the bottle.

"Um…" Mei sounded nervous. "It may be … that I didn't pick up exactly the right sort of shampoo in the shower…"

Before she could say any more there was a roar from the cottage. Jolene stormed out.

"What are you doing? That's twenty-five pounds a bottle. I have to get it shipped from America!" She snatched the shampoo out of Mei's hand. "It's not for animals!"

Jolene stalked back inside. Mei looked at Rose guiltily.

"I'm sorry. I think it might be what makes Jolene's hair red. It is all natural – just, you know, a bit of beetroot and henna added…"

Rose stared at Maltie. He was smothered in red foam. "Oh no! What have we done?"

Rose got her flannel and tried frantically to scrape the foam off. But it was too late. By the time she had managed to sponge the worst of the foam away Maltie's coat no longer had the Dalmatian spots of poo, but it wasn't snowy white either. From nose to bottom, mane to tail, Rose's pony was a perfect candy-floss pink.

"OK, I know about girls doing makeovers but I wasn't expecting that," said Otto.

"He looks like a FLAMINGO," wailed Rose. "How long does it last?"

"Four to six weeks, according to the bottle," muttered Mei, her face turned away.

"SIX WEEKS! What's Miss Pickford going to say when I bring him back pink?"

"He's your pony. It's nothing to do with her," said Mei reasonably. "And he doesn't look like a flamingo; he's got too many legs." She patted Rose's shoulder. "He looks lovely; really..." she searched for the right word, "...special."

"Everyone will stare at us even more," said Rose, unable to stop staring herself.

"Isn't that what Maltie likes best?" Otto pointed: Maltie had caught sight of his reflection in the water trough, and was turning his head one way and then the other. "I reckon Maltie is happy with his new look. That's the most important thing, isn't it?"

Rose wasn't listening. "I'm a walking disaster area."

Maltie *was* happy with his new look. Once he was dry, Rose turned him out in the field and watched him canter up and down by the fence looking very pleased with himself. Glowing like a pat of pink bubble gum, it didn't take long for him to attract attention from passers-by on the bridle path.

A group on horseback were the first to stop. Rose wanted to run away and hide in the yurt as she overheard their exclamations, but she saw Maltie Delight was in his element.

"Excuse me!" One of the riders caught sight of Rose skulking and waved her over. "Is this your pony?"

"Yes," admitted Rose. "He's not normally pink."

"He's gorgeous!" said the girl. "Can I take a selfie with him? It's funny, he looks kind of familiar."

"Oh he loves a selfie, go ahead." Rose sighed and abandoned any hope of anonymity. "He used to be on the telly actually…"

"OMG," said one of the girl's friends. "It's Maltie Delight! From the adverts! It is, isn't it?"

Rose nodded.

"And you won him?"

Rose nodded again. The rider opened her mouth to speak but Rose got in first. "I was very very lucky and my slogan was really nothing special. In fact I don't think I can even remember it now. You can sing him the jingle if you like; he enjoys that."

"Oh yes!" The group burst into song and Maltie obliged with a foot stamp and whinny.

"It's not been the same with that annoying rapping rat," said the first girl.

"He's the lamest thing ever," agreed a boy on a Shetland that he was rather too big for. "It's no wonder the company's in trouble."

"What do you mean?" asked Rose.

"The Good For You Breakfast Cereal Company – they make Maltie Delight, don't they? It's been all over the news. Something about sawdust and rodent droppings found in their muesli. Not good with MD Cheeky..." The boy looked over his shoulder. "Uh-oh, better be quick guys; Miss Brill's coming. We don't want her to catch us up. I can't take any more of her quickfire quizzing."

He loosened his reins and flapped his arms and legs with urgency. The Shetland ambled off.

The girl nodded. "I'm coming. Lovely to meet you Maltie – totally starstruck – you're going straight on my Instagram!" The girl blew a kiss to Maltie, waved to Rose and trotted away.

Before Rose could also disappear, a substantial woman in a blue velvet-trimmed hunting jacket and snowy white jodhpurs came down the path on an even more substantial black horse. A line of smaller riders followed behind her.

"Keep up campers! Ten points and a night off muck-shovelling duties to whoever can name all the points of the horse!" she shouted at them. "Don't keep me waiting! Start with the frog and work up!"

How could a horse also have a frog? wondered Rose. Another pony mystery. She would ask Mei about it later.

"Oh no! Oh no, no, no! Outrageous!" The woman brought her cob to a halt in front of Maltie. She stared at the pony and then at Rose. "Who has desecrated this noble steed? Who has made such mockery of man's oldest helpmeet?"

"It was an accident," said Rose, going pink herself. "It's going to wash out."

"You are not fit to have charge of an equine of excellence. Note this monstrosity children! No adornment or artifice is ever required for a working animal other than the addition of simple plaits for the hunting field or show ring."

Rose, who had never before felt fit to be in charge of any equine, excellent or not, bristled. "I didn't mean to turn him pink but as I think you can see he couldn't be happier about it!"

Maltie had his neck arched and was trotting up and down by the fence, batting his long eyelashes at the line of riders waiting behind Miss Brill. He snorted and pranced and the riders *oohed* and *ahhed*, until quelled by a fierce look from Miss Brill.

"Anyway," said Rose, suddenly feeling braver than usual. "He's my pony. It's nothing to do with you!"

"Well!" It was Miss Brill's turn to snort now. "I have never been spoken to like that. I will not be spoken to like that! You'll come a cropper young lady, that's all I can say! You'll come a cropper!"

Wagging her finger, she thumped her horse's sides with her heels and trotted away. The other riders followed behind, casting wistful looks back at Maltie.

"Too late for that; I already have," said Rose, pulling a face at Miss Brill's back. "Pay no attention my noblest steed and oldest helpmeet; some people are jealous. And rude!"

She stood beside Maltie for a while, breathing in his warm pony smell. He leaned his nose on her shoulder and Rose stroked it idly. It was nice to stand with him in the sun, doing nothing much of anything.

CHAPTER ELEVEN

"Howdy cowhands! It's rodeo day!" said Billy the next morning. "Time to show off your skills while the ponies rest, before we set out for the sea tomorrow."

"You're not going to make us ride Dolly are you?" checked Otto.

"No," said Billy. "I wondered about that but decided Dolly wouldn't be suited."

"Um … Billy, the three of us had a chat about Dolly yesterday evening after the ride out," said Otto tentatively. "We thought it might be better if we don't take her with us on the trail tomorrow. We're not sure she's suited to that either."

Mei and Rose nodded vigorously and made agreeing noises.

To their relief Billy also nodded. "Jolene said the same. She's a good cow is Dolly, but she's not used to being out of her field. It was maybe too exciting for her. I'll have to think some more about managing her before the next group come to Billy's Boots."

"Next group?!" Mei snorted.

"It might be easier if you were on a horse, Billy. Where is your horse?" asked Otto. "What are you riding on the trail tomorrow?"

"Horse? I don't have a hoss. Don't need a hoss to be a cowboy. Just need a cow," said Billy very firmly. "Speaking of which," he continued, "my mate Dave down the village knew a woman who knew a man and so … ta da!"

He proudly pulled a cover off a mound by the fence to reveal a mechanical bull ride: a big brown plastic contraption with horns attached and a saddle seat.

An extension cord trailed away from the base towards the cottage.

"Is that safe?" asked Mei.

"Rodeos aren't meant to be safe," said Billy. "Ah, it'll be fine. Come on! Who wants first try?"

Nobody put their hand up; not even Mei.

"Why don't you show us how it works Billy?" suggested Otto.

"Sure y'all don't mind if I go first?" said Billy. "Can't deny I've been itching to take it for a spin since Dave dropped it round last night." He clambered on top. "Switch on the beast," he called to Jolene, who was standing at the cottage window watching silently.

There was a lot of whirring and creaking. Fans blew into the safety mat underneath the ride and inflated it. Slowly, the bull itself moved. Lurching and tipping, it began to spin round and round.

"It's easy, see?" said Billy, tilting and swaying with the motion. "You hold on tight with one hand, like this, and tip the rest of your weight back, like this, and then keep shifting your centre of gravity, like this. There's a bit of a knack to it of course, so don't expect to find it as easy as I'm making it look. Turn it up a notch Jolene!" he called.

It might have been that the control dial on the second-hand bull ride was sticky and hard to adjust, but Rose thought she glimpsed Jolene smile as she turned it. Whatever the cause, suddenly the bull ride went from rotating in a slow and predictable way to maximum bucking bronco setting. Billy was thrown up and down, side to side and spun at super speed like a banana in a liquidiser.

"Aaaaaaaaaaaaaahhhhhhhhhhhhh!" he screamed. "Tuuuuuurrrrrrrn it dooooowwwwwwwn Joooooooleeeeeeeene!"

"He is very good at holding on," said Mei admiringly.

"Was very good," corrected Otto, as Billy lost his grip. He copied Billy's accent: "And then you fall off, like this."

The safety mat under the mechanical bull was second-hand too. The weight of Billy hitting it at speed squashed all the air out of it. He landed hard on the ground.

The children covered their ears as Billy rolled around swearing.

In a way that was starting to feel familiar, Billy eventually got up off the ground, retrieved his hat and brushed himself down. "Yeah. So that's bull-riding," he said after a silence. "Rodeo's over." He limped off.

"I worry that I don't know what I'm doing, but Billy really doesn't know what he's doing and it doesn't bother him," said Rose. "He's inspirational."

After an afternoon that was supposed to have been spent learning how to line-dance but was actually spent paddling in the river and climbing trees due to the non-appearance of Jolene, Rose rang her parents. "There won't be anywhere to charge my phone on the trail so you won't hear from me for the next couple of days. I'll see you at the pick-up point."

"Hmm? Burminster Sands? By the pier? Yes of course. Don't you worry, we'll be there with the horsebox." Rose's dad sounded distracted.

"You might get a bit of a surprise when you see

Maltie." Rose giggled. "I had an accident with some shampoo. He's sort of gone … pink. I don't know what Miss Pickford will say."

"Accident? Is he too much for you to look after?" Rose's mum came on the phone. "Are you unhappy? Because we can always come and get you both now."

"No Mum! It's fine. We're fine. There's been a few … challenges, that's all. Maltie actually likes being pink. He's so vain, he loves all the people looking at him. Although I wish that didn't mean people then had to look at me too. The pink was half Mei's fault anyway – she gave me the shampoo and—"

Rose's mum broke in. "You know Rose, if you don't like having a pony we should talk about that. Watching you the last few months we've not been sure that this prize has worked out for you. We can easily find Maltie another home if you've had enough. No one will think any less of you for not enjoying a hobby that got pushed on you."

"Alice…" said Rose's dad.

Rose frowned at her phone. What was up with her parents? "I'm OK Mum. It's true that it's not all been that easy I guess…"

"We'll have a chat when we see you and hear all about your adventures properly then," said Rose's dad, sounding more like his normal self. "Enjoy the trail poppet. Can't wait to have you back again. We've missed you so much!"

"Yes! We really have. Good luck and be careful on the trail. Don't mind me – just thinking out loud. See you soon." Rose's mum blew kisses and they hung up.

Rose put the phone down and left the yurt to find Otto and Mei packing saddle bags.

"Billy says just take the essentials," said Mei, handing a bag to Rose. "Jolene's going to bring the tents, sleeping bags and rucksacks to the campsites each night. Or at least he says she is…"

"Maltie won't be impressed at being a pack pony," said Rose.

"He probably thinks a trailer should transport him and all his stuff," said Otto. "You know, the sort rock stars have on tour with heated leather seats, endless champagne and massive tellies."

"With freshly squeezed apple juice on tap and big

mirrors everywhere so he could look at himself all the time." Rose smiled a bit sadly.

"What's the matter?" asked Otto.

"Nothing really. My parents were just saying that I didn't need to keep Maltie. That we could sell him if I wanted to."

"Are they INSANE?" asked Mei. "I would actually die if I didn't have Pepper. And you? You are the luckiest…"

"…lucky person in the world to have won Maltie," Rose finished off for her. "Yes, I know. And even though I've been dumped in mud and sprayed with poo and dyed him pink, these days with Maltie have

been the most fun I've had since I won him. The most fun ever in fact. I guess Carolyn was right that we'd be better on our own away from Plum Orchard. But if my parents had said we could sell him a week ago I'd have leapt at the chance. I was sort of longing to give him up."

"Seriously?"

Rose nodded. "I shouldn't have won Maltie. It was a mistake. There were a million people who deserved him more than me. Who deserve Maltie more than me. He'd be better off with a different owner."

"You can give him to me if you like," said Mei.

"Maybe ..." said Otto, "maybe you learning what it's like to have a pony at the same time as Maltie's finding out what it's like to be a pony – an ordinary one, not a celebrity I mean – maybe that makes you a good match for each other?"

Rose shrugged. "He'd still rather be a celebrity, wouldn't he?"

CHAPTER TWELVE

"This is the life eh? This is the life. Big country skies all around us. Freedom of the trail in front of us. Pioneers crossing the land in search of new horizons."

From his bicycle Billy spread his arm out expansively at the view of farm buildings with corrugated iron roofs, a scrap heap of rusted old machinery parts and the concrete motorway embankment. Rose didn't think it was as magnificent as Billy was selling it, but it was still exciting. They were off on their trail to the sea! A new experience for her and for Maltie Delight.

They were at the back of the ride. Even without a celebrity trailer and entourage, Rose could feel Maltie was bouncy and happy this morning. As they rode on he peeked over hedges curiously and snatched the occasional mouthful of greenery that took his fancy. Now he understood about grass, Maltie was making up for lost time. Rose knew Miss Pickford would disapprove of this habit and did her best to keep her pony focused on walking rather than snacking. She could only hope they wouldn't hit any serious mud or rain to spoil Maltie's good mood.

Directly in front, Dougal lifted his tail and let off a slow series of phutting farts as he plodded.

"Thank you Dougal," said Rose.

"Ah. Not a good idea to be behind me either after days of Billy's cowboy bean diet," said Otto, turning round in his saddle.

"And thank you Otto," added Rose. "I was wondering why the country air didn't seem to smell particularly fresh."

"Sorry," said Otto.

"Hey," called Mei from the front. "There's a log ahead perfect for jumping. Who's coming?"

"I don't think so," said Rose, her shoulders stiffening. She wasn't ready.

"Go on!" Mei encouraged. "You went over that bicycle fine. You'll love it."

"I think I should just watch."

"Suit yourself," said Mei. "Can you look after my saddle bags?"

She unloaded the extra weight, shortened her stirrups a notch and pressed Pepper into a trot, which quickly turned into a canter. Pony and rider flew along the grass and sailed over the tree trunk.

"Jumping isn't really part of the Western riding tradition," said Billy slightly disapprovingly.

"Neither are bicycles," muttered Mei.

"I don't think there's anything to jump in the Wild West. It's all cactuses and canyons isn't it? You wouldn't want to get caught halfway going over either of those," said Otto. "Our turn Dougal."

He took his pony to have a proper look at the log before giving him a good run at it. Dougal also popped over happily.

Rose wondered if she felt a little braver. "What do you think Maltie?" she whispered, stroking his neck and feeling her stomach churn. Maltie was sidling and

dancing, keen to join in with his new friends.
It wasn't a big tree...

"OK. We're doing it." Rose took off Maltie's saddle
bags and shortened her stirrups before she could
change her mind.

They cantered towards the jump. Rose felt a
moment of panic. The log loomed in front like a
two metre-high solid brick wall.

"I don't think I should. I don't think I can..."
she began – and then suddenly Maltie was up and
over, and Rose was right there with him. His pink
mane flew up as her stomach somersaulted. It was
a wonderful feeling.

"Oh!" said Rose.

"Fun see?" said Mei.
"Want another go?"

And Rose found
that she
did.

When everyone had finished jumping they rode on further until they reached an open grassy slope. An old oak tree stood in the middle offering shade and Billy decided this would be a good spot to stop for lunch. They unsaddled the ponies and brought apples and squashed sandwiches out from their bags.

With their tack off and tethered on long ropes to graze, Dougal and Pepper took the opportunity to lie down and roll blissfully on the grass. Maltie watched them curiously.

"Why don't you give rolling a go too Maltie?" suggested Rose. "It's quite dry here. You won't get muddy."

Maltie half dropped to his front knees and put his head and neck on the grass experimentally, then changed his mind and pushed back up. He looked uncharacteristically unsure of himself.

"Go on! You can do it!" encouraged Rose.

Maltie went down again, this time all the way. He rolled over onto his back and rubbed backwards and forwards on the grass, kicking his pink legs in the air in a rather undignified manner.

"That's the way!" said Rose. Otto and Mei cheered. Maltie pushed himself back up and snorted. He shook his whole body like a wet dog and then swung his mane around in a deceptively casual way. "You see? You didn't get muddy and I bet that felt great. I'm very proud of you Maltie," Rose added, patting him reassuringly. She gave him a piece of her apple.

After lunch they continued along the bridleway. When that came to an end they walked down the side of a country lane. Traffic on its way to a car boot sale backed up behind them. Billy waved the cars past and there were curious looks from drivers and passengers as they took in Maltie's pink coat. Rose felt self-conscious and kept her gaze straight ahead between her pony's ears, but as ever Maltie loved the attention. Some people recognised him and wound down their windows to sing. He turned his head to each one and pranced a little on the tarmac to give them the best possible view of his beauty.

Rose concentrated on staying in control, anticipating his foot stamps and whinnies. "Yes, you are gorgeous but settle down Maltie," she muttered, putting her hand on his neck.

"Does he do hoofographs?" asked one driver. In answer Maltie lifted his tail and dropped balls of poo along the road. The driver laughed. "I should be picking those up to sell at the car boot eh? Famous manure! Now you'd not mistake one of those for a raisin in your morning cereal."

Rose was relieved when they left the road but Maltie snorted in disappointment at losing his audience. The path now passed between fields and into a wood. Billy had to get off and push his bicycle and Rose had to use all her skill to get a sulking Maltie past squelchy sections and round mane-catching branches. When they finally came back out into sunshine they were on the brow of a hill, and the view opened up all around them. It was a patchwork of roads and fields and villages with church spires.

"Where's the sea?" asked Mei, shielding her eyes to stare at the horizon.

"Still miles away I think," said Otto.

"There's a way to go yet," agreed Billy. "Our first evening camp isn't so far away though. Could probably see that from here." He frowned.

Rose stretched her legs out of her stirrups. To her surprise she didn't feel saddle sore. She felt warm and loose. She'd been using her brain almost as much as her body to keep in touch with Maltie all day; it had made her a good sort of tired. She caught sight of her arms. They were turning golden and freckled from being outdoors all the time, despite the factor fifty sunscreen her mum had packed.

"Where are we camping tonight Billy?" Otto raised an eyebrow. "Hope it's got protection from wild

coyotes and bandits."

Billy scratched his nose. "Thought we could hunker down and pitch our wagons wherever we found ourselves at sundown, but Jolene says that's against the law. Rang around some campsites. They weren't much help. Trickier than I thought to find a place that will take hosses."

"We have got somewhere to stay haven't we?" asked Mei.

"Course we have," said Billy tersely. "Another five miles or so to go. Jolene sorted it. We're camping in Bobby's back garden. He's an old friend – used to be our manager." Billy set his mouth and stroked his chin. His eyes narrowed as he gazed out at the view. "Better get going I guess. Downhill from here at least." He climbed onto his bicycle and freewheeled away.

CHAPTER THIRTEEN

"Welcome! Welcome! Come and make yourselves comfortable down in the orchard. Everything you need should be there."

A plummy-voiced man in a black polo neck beckoned them off the road and through tall wrought-iron gates. "Good to see you Billy; what a reunion! Keeping well with your new project?" The man smirked at Billy's limp and collection of plasters and bandages as he ushered them down the driveway.

It was a very grand driveway. When Billy had said they were camping in a back garden, Rose had imagined a rectangle of lawn lined with flowerbeds. She'd wondered how they would fit. But back garden here meant acres of grass freshly striped by

 a lawnmower, sweeping down to a lake and orchards beyond. It was more like a stately home. There was even a fountain and some stone statues nestled in the tall green hedges. Maltie put his head up and trotted more smartly, showing off with his best mane twirl to the man as he passed. Rose could tell her pony approved of this campsite.

"Bobby did well for himself," said Billy as they led the ponies through to the orchard. He had never looked more like an inscrutable cowboy.

In the orchard, the tents and equipment had been left piled on the grass. There was no sign of Jolene. Otto, Mei and Rose untacked and rubbed down the ponies and let them loose to graze before putting up the tents. Rose was relieved to see that the yurt wasn't there and she had exactly the same as the others this time.

As they were pegging out the guy ropes, the glass

doors at the back of the house opened and Jolene came out. She wandered across the lawn and made her way down to them. She looked very different. She was dressed in an evening gown and rhinestone cowboy boots and had a glass of champagne in one hand. Even more dramatically, she was smiling.

"How was your ride? Come inside Billy. We need to talk: Bobby and me been catching up. He's got plans."

"I don't know," said Billy, looking awkward. "I've never had much to say to Bobby, Jolene. I need to get the campfire going and the beans on."

"We can start the fire Billy," said Rose.

"And cook our tea," said Otto, peering into a cool box and carrier bags.

Billy rubbed his neck. "It's not really in the spirit of the trail to go indoors."

Mei patted his arm. "It's not really in the spirit of the trail to camp in a garden either. Nobody cares. Go. We know where to find you if there's a problem."

Billy shrugged, adjusted his hat and followed Jolene back up the garden.

Rose collected some twigs and dry moss and made a

pyramid of kindling in the fire pit at the edge of the orchard.

"Are you going to slosh on petrol now?" asked Mei.

"No," said Rose. She lit a single match and, cupping the flame, placed it in the heart of the dry moss. It glowed and smouldered and, as Rose blew gently, the flame took hold and the fire licked into life. Rose sat back on her haunches, pleased with herself.

"That was easy," said Otto, coming over with a bag.

"I did scouts for a term," said Rose. "What have you got there?"

"Dinner!" said Otto. "Eggs and a tin of potatoes and onions. I'm going to cook us a potato omelette thing."

"Not beans?"

"Totally bean free. Although there are six cans of beans if you want some?"

"I'm good," said Rose quickly. "You know how to cook?"

"I like cooking. I can do eggs and I can do pasta. And toast and milkshakes. And that's all anyone needs," said Otto. He began to break eggs into a metal bowl and mix them with a fork. Rose put a grate over one edge of the fire and found a frying pan in one of the bags.

It got burned around the edges but Otto's potato omelette thing was still the best food Rose and Mei had ever eaten. They licked their plates completely clean like proper cowboys, then took it in turns to feed new pieces of wood into the fire and watch the flames dance. As the sun went down they grinned at each other. They could hear their ponies cropping grass in the shadows beyond where the tents were pitched. On the other side the house glowed with light. Music was playing and occasionally there was a raised voice or a shout of laughter.

"That was a fun day but the fire's made me sleepy. I'm going to bed," announced Mei with a yawn as the flames died down.

"There's still no sign of Billy. Did you see him when you went to use the toilet?" asked Rose. "Do you think he's OK?"

"Isn't it supposed to be his job to check on us? The door was closed but I heard Jolene singing. She's pretty good."

Rose got ready to go to bed too. It felt strange to be in a small tent without space to stand up after the yurt, but it was cosier. She snuggled down into her sleeping bag and drifted off, dimly aware of the faintest pitter-patter of raindrops beginning to fall on the canvas above her head.

THRRIIIPPPPP!

Rose woke with a lurch. Beneath her the ground was erupting, all her possessions sliding to one side of the tent. Was there an earthquake?

"Maltie! What are you doing? YOU CAN'T FIT IN THIS ONE!"

Her pony's head poked under the zip of the tent. Pegs popped. Maltie pulled back and the whole tent came with him, ripping out of the ground.

"Help!" Rose found herself being shaken down the canvas and banging into Maltie, who was blocking the door, trying to force himself inside. Trapped, she struggled to unzip the side window instead, somersaulted through it still in her sleeping bag, and hopped sack race-style round to extract Maltie from his

flapping tent-
cape-hat.
"You can't
wear a tent
you numpty."

There had
to be another
place to shelter.
It was raining quite hard.
Rose got out of her sleeping bag and retrieved her
wellies and coat from the collapsed tent.

"Come with me you great pink pain-in-the-bum of
a pony." Rose took hold of Maltie's head collar and
led him quietly away from the camp and out through
the orchard gate. They walked around the ornamental
lake, Rose feeling guilty about dotting the neat lawn
with muddy horse-shoe prints. There was a stone
summer house built in the style of a Greek temple on
the other side. It had just enough room for them to fit
under its roof and keep dry.

Rose spread out her sleeping bag on a bench
next to a pair of kissing stone cherubs. Maltie stood

beside her, his neck drooped and one hoof tipped up as he settled down to doze. Rose reached out from her sleeping bag and put her hand against his solid, slightly steamy neck. He was much more comforting than her old teddy. She left her hand where it was, closed her eyes and went back to sleep.

"Darling!" A plummy voice woke Rose. "Hand me my phone! This would make a perfect cover shot for a comeback album – it's the concept we've been searching for all night Jo-Jo! I can see it now: 'Unicorn Dreams'. That's your title."

Rose sat up to find Bobby and Jolene right in front of her. It didn't look like either of them had been to bed. Jolene was still in her evening gown. Bobby was taking photos on his phone while Maltie posed, snorting and pawing the ground. The early morning sunlight shining into the temple was making Maltie's pink coat appear almost luminous: a pony-sized pink highlighter pen.

"This horse is a true professional – real star quality. I could make use of a pony like this," Bobby enthused.

Rose blearily held an arm in front of her puffy face. Personally she wasn't ready for a photo shoot. "Where's Billy?"

"Billy?" Jolene shrugged. "I don't know. Bobby and I have been writing songs all night. Billy and me are finished anyway. I told him that this time I'm going solo. I'm through with country living."

"Ah dear Billy." Bobby shook his head. "But darling, if it hadn't been for his camp we'd have missed the once-in-a-blue-moon creative spark that hit last night. There was magic in the air. Your voice! Those melodies! Come back to the house and I'll make coffee. We've got a lot of phone calls to make to get you back in the studio."

Rose led Maltie back to the orchard.

"We were wondering where you'd disappeared to. What happened to your tent?" asked Otto. "Can you help get the fire going again so we can cook bacon for breakfast?"

"Have you seen Billy?" asked Rose.

"He's in there," said Mei, indicating Billy's tent with her head. "He said he didn't want to be disturbed."

"Hmm," said Rose. "I think he's had a tricky night with Jolene. Today may not go to plan."

"Well THAT will make a change," said Mei.

CHAPTER FOURTEEN

"Which way now Billy?" Mei asked yet again.

"I'm sure we've passed that tree stump before," said Rose.

"Shouldn't we be reaching tonight's camp soon?" prodded Otto.

A dishevelled and silent Billy had emerged from his tent mid-morning. They'd packed up camp and he'd cycled furiously away from Bobby's house, making them all trot to keep up as they passed through farmland and along a series of rough tracks. But as the final track had petered out, Billy's pace and anger had ebbed away. For the last few hours they'd been ambling, picking their way through open countryside, and Billy was worryingly quiet.

"It's not right..." mumbled Billy at last.

"OK," said Mei, turning Pepper. "Left then."

"Left me!" continued Billy. "She's left me! It's not right." He got off his bike and threw it down onto the grass. "What's the point?"

Rose halted Maltie. "Are we lost Billy?"

"We're all lost – apart from Jolene that is," said Billy. Mei rolled her eyes. "She found herself again by Bobby's piano last night and says she doesn't need a Mustang Boy any more. What happened to our dreams Jolene! Who's going to run the yoga retreats now?" he shouted at the sky. "I don't know how to do yoga." His shoulders slumped.

"You don't know how to be a cowboy but that hasn't stopped you starting a Wild West riding camp," pointed out Mei.

"Perhaps Jolene's dreams were a bit different to yours," Rose said, trying to be gentle.

"Where were we supposed to camp tonight Billy?"asked Otto."Your phone is charged isn't it? We could call Jolene or somebody else for help."

"Took a brick to my phone last night. Jolene's face

was the screensaver. Jolene's voice was the ringtone," Billy answered.

There was a short silence, broken by some far from sympathetic groaning from Mei.

"We're camping with Jonny's donkeys, down near Littleleigh beach," Billy said.

"Finally," said Mei. "So where's that?"

Billy shrugged.

"We can't be too far away," said Rose, sniffing the air. There was a brisk breeze. "I can smell sea salt. If we head in one direction we're sure to come to a road or a house eventually. It's not like we're in the real Wild West wilderness." Rose squinted at the sky. "We should keep the sun on our right."

"What sun?" asked Otto. He had a point: an increasing amount of cloud was blowing across the sky, scooting in low.

They walked on, doing their best to navigate and stopping every so often to wait for Billy, who trailed behind pushing his bicycle. The clouds got thicker and thicker and lower and lower. It became impossible not just to track the sun but to see anything or anyone at all. Only the strengthening salty tang in the air encouraged them to keep going.

"This is a proper sea mist. We must be close," said Rose, trying to look for positives. Maltie trotted forward, leading the way.

"I can't see anything," complained Mei as the pinkish tinge of Maltie's bottom vanished in the porridge-thick whiteness.

"Help!" came Rose's sudden shout, with an echoing whinny from Maltie and the sound of tumbling rocks.

"Rose! ROSE! Are you all right?" called Mei. She swung herself out of her saddle, handed Pepper's reins to Otto and stumbled through the fog.

She found Rose and Maltie quivering, looking down at where the land fell away into a white void of nothingness below. The roar of waves crashing against rocks beneath confirmed they'd found the sea at last. They backed away from the edge.

"We nearly went over the cliff," said Rose shakily. "Maltie stopped just in time. He saved us."

"Clever pony; not just a pretty face," said Mei. "And not just puddles he stops for."

"What now?" said Otto. "We can't carry on in this."

"We can't stop either," said Mei. "We'll freeze."

"And starve – there's no food left," said Otto gloomily. "What do you think we should do Rose?"

Rose was surprised to be deferred to. "There must be a cliff path we could follow. We need to go very, very slowly."

There was the squeaking of a bicycle wheel as Billy finally caught up with them. "Should be careful, there'll be cliffs near by," he offered helpfully.

Dismounting, every one of Rose's muscles ached. She felt scared too. What if they didn't reach any houses before dark? Her eyes blurred with tears. Beside her Maltie whickered gently and nudged her shoulder. Rose gulped. She couldn't despair, she had a responsibility to her pony. He'd just saved her life. Together, they'd be all right. They began to walk.

"Did you hear that?" A little further on Rose stopped, catching something over the top of the wind and sea sounds.

"What?" said Mei.

"Sssh … wait … there?"

"Yes!" said Otto."Shout everyone. Shout! HALLLOOOOO! HELP!"

In reply came the sound again, clearer now: "Hee-haw! Hee-haw!"

"Cream on your hot chocolate and ketchup with your egg? How did you sleep?"

"Like a forest of logs," said Rose, emerging from her tent. "Yes please to cream and no to ketchup. Thanks Jonny." She took the plate and mug that the grey-bearded man was holding out to her.

"What about your pink pony? He need anything? Looks like he should be on a carousel."

"Don't worry, I'll look after him," said Rose, looking over at Maltie. She was surprised to see him grazing happily with his new companions. She hadn't been sure how Maltie Delight, Very Important Pony, would cope with sharing an overnight paddock with donkeys. But it seemed he was as relieved as the rest of them to have found Jonny and not to have spent the night on a cold, foggy cliff.

"Now this is what I call a trail camp," Mei had

said when they'd arrived to find their tents already pitched and hot fish and chips waiting for them. But Billy had been devastated all over again when Jonny had broken the news that Jolene had dumped the stuff and disappeared.

"How's Billy this morning?" Rose asked Jonny now.

Jonny shook his head. "Not too bright. Daft idea this holiday scheme of his but he's always been full of those. Last time it was an ostrich farm. Ten of them got out and went running wild on the motorway as I remember. Jolene and he had a bust-up then too. But Billy's got a good heart."

"I suppose we can't finish the trail on our own," said Rose sadly.

"Don't see why not," said Jonny. "You've come all this way, you've got to finish. I'll set the three of you on the right path when I take my girls down to the beach. It's not too tricky."

Breakfast finished, Jonny saddled up his donkeys. Each had a brightly coloured cloth put on before their saddles. Their bridles were decorated with felt tassels

and
flowers
and had
their names
on their
nosebands:
Caroline and
Coco, Mabel and

Queenie. Maltie stared at them with envy.

As Jonny handed out packed lunches, Billy came to the doorway of the cottage, tear-stained and huddled in a blanket. "Sorry if the holiday wasn't what you were expecting. I still had a few details to work on and then... JOLENE!" His voice choked.

"Don't worry Billy. We've had a really interesting time," said Rose.

They set off, clattering down the road ."Donkeys and me only going as far as Littleleigh," explained Jonny. "Got a pitch next to the beach huts. From there you'll follow the coast path back up along the cliffs and then down to Burminster Sands. The car park's next to the pier at the end. I've rung your parents and told them to meet you there, reassured them you won't get lost. Have any of your horses been near the sea before?"

Rose, Mei and Otto all shook their heads.

"We'll see how they get on at Littleleigh. You can help me out with the first customers of the day."

Jonny's donkeys turned off the road and on to a boardwalk through the dunes. Their long, soft ears pricked up and they started to jog as they recognised their route.

"All right you lot! Think there's treats to come do you? Maybe you're right." Jonny patted Queenie's velvet neck.

Picking up on the donkey's excitement the ponies began to jog too, snorting at the unfamiliar tang of salt and the noise of the waves getting closer. At the end of the boardwalk they all saw it at once: a green-grey, froth-topped line stretching out to the horizon. The sea! Maltie plunged his head up and down. Pepper gave a small buck. Even Dougal began to dance.

A small crowd was already gathered on the beach,

waiting for donkey rides. They were excited to see the new additions.

"Look Mum! A PINK donkey!" said one small boy, tugging at his mum's arm excitedly. "I wanna ride the PINK donkey!"

His older sister was withering. "That's not a donkey. That's a unicorn. It's too big for you." Her eyes widened."Can I ride that one Mum?"

"He's not a unicorn," Rose corrected as Jonny started loading up the donkeys with their first passengers. "He hasn't got a horn, see?"

"Can he fly then? Is he like Pegasus?" the girl suggested.

"No wings either. He's just a pony. Although he did used to be on the television. His name's Maltie Delight..." There were *oohs* and *ahhhs*. "He's gone pink because I washed him wrong," explained Rose.

"That happened to my school shirt too. Did you put a red sock in the machine with him?"

"I don't think he'll mind if you want to have a short turn on him." Rose slipped off her pony's back and helped one of the children scramble on in her place.

Maltie kept very still and turned his head so that he was showing his best profile while the child's parents took hundreds of pictures.

After that everyone wanted a go. Maltie was perfectly behaved as different toddlers were put on him, all of them howling when they were taken off again. Rose felt super proud. She would never have expected her pony to be so good-natured about hanging out with donkeys and tiny children. Some of them had quite grubby fingers. It was probably just as well Maltie couldn't see what they were smearing on his mane.

"He makes a grand donkey," said Jonny, chuckling. "Let me know if you ever want to sell him."

CHAPTER FIFTEEN

The three pairs of pony and rider were set back on the cliff path by Jonny and walked the last few miles together, feeling free. The end of their camping adventure was in sight.

"Would you rather have had a proper organised holiday at that Miss Brill's place and done her pony quizzes?" Otto asked.

"No WAY," said Mei. "I like doing things, not answering questions about things."

"Maltie might have preferred it. He'd have had a proper stable, and I bet Miss Brill doesn't allow any mud in her yard." Rose stretched down and put her arms around her pink pony's neck. Maltie flicked his ears back and forth. "But I wouldn't have liked it half as much."

"It's been very good for Maltie, mixing with the other half," observed Otto. "Dougal's taught him lots about how to let go and enjoy being a pony – haven't you Dougal?" Dougal lifted his tail and let go of a trail of poo. "Maltie will be rolling right in muddy puddles before you know it."

"And you've both taught me lots about riding. Thank you," said Rose, flushing red. Everyone looked a bit embarrassed. "Oh, look!" Rose said quickly, pointing out to sea. "The pier!"

Mei trotted ahead and called back, "The turning to Burminster Sands is just here. Jonny said we're allowed to canter on that beach."

"I don't suppose Maltie will want to get his hooves wet," said Rose, half relieved and half wistful.

They picked their way carefully down a twisty path lined with yellow gorse that smelled deliciously of coconuts. At the bottom the sand was smooth and inviting. It was a beautiful beach, almost empty apart from a few figures walking dogs or picking up shells towards the other end. The waves were long and low, and as each pulled away the wet sand shone back the blue of the sky. The ponies began to snort and jog again.

"This is what I've been waiting for. Come on Pepper!" Mei urged her pony forward. They hit the firm damp sand and Pepper needed no more encouragement. She cantered straight into the surf, her hooves kicking up a spray of diamonds as they raced along the water's edge.

"Whoopeeeeeeee!" hollered Mei, her voice fading on the wind.

"Ready?" Otto asked Rose.

"You go," said Rose.

As Dougal cantered away Maltie was as keen to follow as ever. Rose took a deep breath and hastily shortened her reins to keep contact. If she fell off at least the landing would be soft and clean this time. "OK! It's going to be cold Maltie – are you sure you want to?"

Maltie, already jogging, sprang into a canter at Rose's first suggestion. He stretched his neck forward, lengthened his stride and took off. Rose, who had hardly been brave enough to stroke a horse only a few months previously, found herself galloping on her very own pony and with her new very best friends along the edge of foamy rolling waves. Little flecks of sand and water

splashed up and
speckled her clothes
and Maltie's sides.
She didn't care – and
miraculously, neither
did Maltie. His
ears were pricked,
his hooves pounded
a thrilling drum beat
and his mane and tail
rippled out in the wind
like pink streamers. It
was like flying; pure
magic. I can ride! Rose
thought, I can really ride!

As the pier loomed closer and the
beach began to run out, Rose reluctantly sat back in
her saddle and brought Maltie back to a walk. She
circled him around on a loose rein and went to meet
Mei and Otto at the edge of the sand. They were both
glowing and grinning as much as her.

"I would just like to say—" Rose stretched down

to pat Maltie's damp, steaming neck— "that I am the luckiest, lucky person that ever lived." For once Rose absolutely knew it was true.

"Rose? Rose! Yoo-hoo ROSE!" Two figures were hurrying along the sand. Rose swung out of her saddle and went to meet her parents. They hugged her tightly.

"Look at you! Look at you! You're ten years older," said Rose's mum, squishing her cheeks.

"Not quite," laughed Rose.

"We missed you. We didn't like being on our own," said her dad. He glanced at Maltie. "Goodness, your nag is pink isn't he? Quite a change in both of you."

"Miss Pickford's going to be furious I expect," said Rose but she smiled. Her stomach no longer churned at the thought. "She'll just have to lump it." Rose caught her mum and dad exchanging glances. Her dad gave a tiny shake of his head. "What?"

Her dad clapped his hands together. "Right! Who's for an ice cream? Mei and Otto, is it? There are two more horseboxes in the car park; your parents are waiting there too. I'll stand a round for everybody. We heard from Jonny that the week hasn't gone quite to plan, so I reckon you've all earned them."

"Thanks Mr Steggles," said Otto. "It's definitely been quite a holiday."

"I'm just relieved that you've all made it out the other end in one piece. I'm going to be sending a lot of emails when we get home," said Rose's mum.

"For all the good they'll do under the circumstances," she added more quietly.

There were ice creams on the pier and crunchy mint sticks of Burminster rock that exactly matched the colour of Maltie's coat for the ponies. Everyone's parents shook hands and shared a grumble about Billy.

When it was time to say goodbye, Otto nudged his father. "Dad?"

"Oh yes, I'm on it Otto..." Otto's dad turned to Rose's and Mei's parents. "Otto's wondering if your girls and their ponies would like to come down to ours for the weekend soon? There's not a lot of space indoors, but if the weather's kind there's plenty of space outdoors for them to camp and it's great countryside for riding. They'd be very welcome, and I promise we'd look after them properly."

"Yes. I'm coming," said Mei very definitely.

Her mother rolled her eyes. "Mei!" Rose could see the family resemblance. She looked over at her own parents.

"Thank you, that's a really kind offer," said her dad, looking uncomfortable. "There's just one or two things we're going to need to discuss with Rose first though."

"It's time we were heading home," said Rose's mum. "It's a long drive, especially when you're not used to pulling a horsebox. But getting the kids together one way or another sounds a great idea. We'll be in touch."

Rose, Otto and Mei gave each other awkward hugs goodbye.

"I don't know what's up with my parents. They're not normally like that," said Rose.

"WhatsApp us," said Mei. "I want to see photos of Maltie at Plum Orchard. And be brave with all the other riders there! You know we're not that scary now..."

Rose stuck her tongue out. "I will! See you soon, I hope."

Maltie, Dougal and Pepper exchanged gentle nostril snorts and then Rose led her pony up the ramp into his horsebox.

"Are you going to tell me what's going on?" she asked her parents once they'd set off.

"Perhaps it should wait until we're home," said her mum. "You must be exhausted and longing for your own bed."

"Now," said Rose with unusual firmness. "I want to hear whatever it is now."

Her dad glanced back at her and then stared out the windscreen, gripping the steering wheel tightly. "We'd hoped you wouldn't be too bothered, all things considered. It's not like you were ever expecting to win Maltie Delight and it's been a bit of a bind having to spend all that time at the stables, hasn't it? That Miss Pickford is a right dragon, eh?" He laughed nervously.

"We had a call from Miss Pickford after you left," Rose's mum took over. "It seems Maltie's stable bill and your lesson costs haven't actually been settled. I tried to get hold of that Davina PR woman but she was 'unavailable'."

"She's probably not been paid herself, to be fair," said Rose's dad. "The Good For You Breakfast Cereal Company declared bankruptcy two days ago, Rose. The papers are saying they spent too much on the rebrand and now they've been hit with a massive lawsuit for things turning up in their muesli that aren't listed on the ingredients."

"Your prize contract turns out to have more holes than a bath sponge. Your father should never have signed it so hastily. If I'd had a chance to properly look at it I could have made sure that—"

"Not again Alice! The problem is, Rose, that we're now having to pay a very hefty bill to Miss Pickford for the last few months. And we had no idea that owning a pony would be anything like as expensive as it is."

"I see," said Rose. A nugget of ice seemed to have frozen up her throat.

"I'm sorry, poppet. We're glad you've had a fun week but we're really going to have to think hard about how we can manage that long term," said her mum.

"Of course, we can always find a way. Make some economies at home. Save money on holidays, and the car could go perhaps..." began her dad.

Rose broke in. "Don't worry Dad. I understand."

She held her voice steady. "You're right: I never wanted to be a rider anyway." Rose stared hard out of the window at the countryside rushing past. "We should put Maltie up for sale, shouldn't we? That's the best thing to do."

"Are you sure Rosie Pose?" said her dad, but Rose caught her parents exchanging a relieved glance.

"Quite sure," said Rose. Somehow she managed a smile to her dad in the rear view mirror. "I'm totally fine."

"That's a weight off our minds," said her mum with a sigh. "No need to rush into anything. We'll

make sure we find him the perfect home, we promise, love. Actually, Miss Pickford has already offered to help with that."

"Oh I'm sure Miss Pickford will be able to find a much more suitable owner than me for Maltie," said Rose. It took her no effort to sound like she believed it. After all, she'd always known it wasn't supposed to be her. She wasn't the kind of person a pony like Maltie happened to.

CHAPTER SIXTEEN

Finding Maltie a better owner took Miss Pickford a fortnight. She stopped Rose and Carolyn in the yard one Saturday morning.

"Lavinia Cholmely-Pye is coming at two to try your mount. See that he's looking his best, in so far as that is possible given his ridiculous colour." The riding instructor stalked off.

Rose's one-on-one lessons with Miss Pickford had come to an abrupt stop after Rose and Maltie's awkward return from camp. Instead Rose and her pony had taken to going out on bittersweet hacks exploring the countryside together. They'd also joined Carolyn's group lessons, where Sian Hamill and the other riders had been more friendly than before. Rose suspected this was partly out of sympathy and partly from glee that her luck had run out.

Rose's parents had promised they'd continue paying for these lessons after Maltie was sold. Rose hadn't told them or Carolyn she wouldn't be doing that. She wouldn't ride again once Maltie had gone. What would be the point without Maltie?

"You don't have to stay this afternoon," Carolyn said to Rose now. Although Rose had done her very best to put on a calm and resigned face about Maltie's sale, Carolyn seemed to have guessed that wasn't the full story. "I can sort out Maltie and meet the Cholmely-Pyes. If Lavinia likes him, she and her grooms will take good care of him, I'm sure. They're a famously horsey family. Lavinia has three other top show ponies already."

"No, I'll stay," said Rose. "She sounds like his dream owner and I should make Maltie look his best. I'll even plait his mane. First impressions are important."

Rose sighed, remembering how Maltie had curled his lip at her unbrushed hair and milk-stained school uniform when they'd first met.

Maltie didn't seem to mind her tired eyes and faded T-shirt when Rose entered his stable now. He whickered a greeting and gently biffed her shoulder, snuffling hopefully against her coat pocket for a minty treat. Rose found one  and leaned into him briefly as he ate it, breathing in the smell of his warm neck. She had to force herself to step away, fetch the brushes, comb, elastic bands and hoof oil and get to work. She would show her pony at his best, even if it broke her heart.

"Oh my goodness! What a sight!"

Despite Rose's best efforts, Lavinia Cholmely-Pye still giggled when Maltie Delight was brought out for inspection a few hours later. Rose bristled: Maltie's plaits might be a bit bulky and coming loose, but she had managed to polish his hindquarters to a beautiful sheen and his tail was snag free and billowing. The pink had faded and Maltie's coat was now a subtle blush-rosebud tinge, nothing like as bright as it had been.

"Can't say Miss P didn't warn us. What do you think Mum? Better than the palomino we saw at Newmarket?" The girl ignored Rose as she squinted at Maltie.

"Nice chest and hocks, Lavvy, and you need a foil to your chestnuts and bays to keep catching the judges' eyes," said the woman beside her. Both Lavinia and Mrs Cholmely-Pye were immaculately turned-out in waxed jackets, white jodhpurs and spotless boots. "Plus we can negotiate a bargain price, all things considered."

Rose wanted to cover Maltie Delight's ears so he couldn't hear the outrage of the word "bargain" being used about him.

"I'll try his paces. Miss Pickford says he's well-schooled but I'm sure he'll have picked up plenty of bad habits from the novice. We can put him in a double bridle if necessary."

"Nothing you can't fix, Lavvy. Your seat is second to none."

"True." Lavinia looked at Rose and smiled condescendingly. "Thanks, I'll take him from here."

She grabbed the reins and led Maltie away. Rose watched him go, her throat constricted and her heart pounding. Softly, she began to sing:

"Maltie Delight. The bowl to start your day right. Keep trotting from morning to night…"

Hearing her, Maltie stopped and turned, stomped his feet and whinnied happily. Unable to hold them back one minute longer, Rose burst into tears and ran straight out of Plum Orchard Riding Stables.

Safely in her bedroom, Rose let yet more tears fall while Mei and Otto offered long-distance support on WhatsApp.

Mei
LAVINIA CHOLMELY-PYE?? You CAN'T sell to her. You can't. She came to a show down our way with a whole lorry full of ponies and won EVERYTHING. She's awful!

Otto
She beat you Mei?

Mei
That's not my point. You tell Rose.

Otto
Don't give up Rose. There's got to be a way to keep Maltie.

Rose read their messages and shook her head. Didn't they understand?

> **Rose**
> I'm NOT giving up! He'll be happier with Lavinia. She's a brilliant rider and she lives in a stately home with loads of stables and grooms and everything. No mud. He'll love it.
>
> **Otto**
> No he won't. He'll be one of loads of beautiful and talented ponies and that'll make him look ordinary, won't it? He won't like that at ALL.

Rose sat up. She hadn't thought of that. Maltie definitely wouldn't enjoy being one of a crowd if everyone else also showed off and no one was impressed by his breakfast cereal past. Hope flared briefly before reality hit again.

> **Rose**
> So what do you expect me to do about it? It's alright for both of you. You can keep Dougal and Pepper at your homes. There's no space for him in our garden.
>
> **Mei**
> If only we lived closer.
>
> **Otto**
> Talk to your parents. Livery doesn't have to be expensive if you look after Maltie and turn him out in the summer.

> **Rose**
> I know but there's already a huge debt to pay off. And shoes and hay and vet fees. I can't ask. Even if they agreed I'd feel guilty all the time.

Her fingers paused before typing again.

> **Rose**
> I'm ALREADY guilty about the amount of money they spent having me.
>
> **Otto**
> ???
>
> **Rose**
> They had to have loads of treatment to get pregnant with me. It took years of injections and preparations and test-tubes and I cost thousands. They got a loan from the bank. And look what they got!

Rose threw down her phone and let more quiet tears flow into her long-suffering pillow. She could hear her parents moving around downstairs, murmuring as they prepared dinner together. She'd never told anyone about that before: all those almost-babies, but it was only her – Rose, who wasn't brave or clever or popular – who'd been the one to make it. She loved her parents. She wouldn't ask them to make even more sacrifices for a prize that, only a few weeks ago, she hadn't even wanted.

Her phone pinged again with a new message. Rose picked it up, prepared to argue with whatever kind words Otto had sent her, but the message was from Mei. In characteristic Mei style it was to the point.

Mei
Sell something. Get a job.

Rose didn't type anything back, but she did wipe her eyes. "Yeah right Mei. A paper round's not going to be enough," she said to her phone. She looked around her room. She would happily sell her ridiculous only-worn-once riding jacket, but that wouldn't do it either.

"Dinner's ready Rosie!" her mum called up the stairs. "*Make Me A Superstar*'s on afterwards."

"Coming," Rose called back as brightly as she could. She blew her nose. Soon Maltie would be off to his new life, and watching the singers try out on *Make Me A Superstar* with her parents would be all the excitement she could expect. It had once been enough.

Surely it could be again?

As she got off her bed, the thought of singers made Rose pause, struck by a memory from camp. If she couldn't get a job that would pay enough to keep Maltie, could there be another way?

CHAPTER SEVENTEEN

Rose had thought it would be a difficult phone call. To her relief Billy sounded quite cheerful.

"I'm doing better thanks Rose. I've sold up and I'm moving to Arizona next month. Got a real cowboy job on a dude ranch!"

"Wow, that's great Billy!" Rose hoped the ranch wasn't expecting a fully trained cowboy. "What's going to happen to Dolly and the ducks?"

"Jonny's got room for them in his field. Dolly will get on well with the donkeys."

"And…" this was the part that Rose had to approach carefully, "how are things with Jolene?"

Billy let out a long sigh. "Spoke to her about selling our stuff. She's moved back to London, to start again with her music. Got some big crunch meeting with the record company coming up. I feel calmer about our split now. We had grown apart. Can you credit it: she told me she never wanted to run a holiday camp in the first place?!" Billy's voice was disbelieving.

Rose tried to be tactful. "Yes, I think we all got that impression. Actually I was hoping that I might be able to speak to Jolene and Bobby about something. Have you got any contact details for her?" She crossed her fingers.

"I can give you her phone number," said Billy. "But you won't get anything out of her until next week. She and Bobby are locked in the studio recording. She won't speak to anyone until the tracks are down and the contract is signed."

Rose uncrossed her fingers, her heart sinking. Next week would be too late. Everything had been sorted for Lavinia to collect Maltie next Sunday. There was only one thing for it – and it was going to require the sort of determination Rose couldn't think about without feeling dizzy.

"Do you know where the studio is, Billy?"

* * *

There was a lot to organise.

Mei

We're meeting at 10.30 right? I've got train tickets and the Google Map link. And I'll bring the other stuff we need.

Rose

Was your mum OK about the idea of a day trip? Will you be able to get away from her?

Mei

She's amazed I agreed to spend a Saturday away from Pepper. I've got to do boring shopping for bridesmaid shoes later. But she says I can spend a couple of hours with you as long as I've got my phone.

Otto

My brother's agreed to pick us up with the trailer and drop you home at the end Rose. He's having all my Sunday roast potatoes and first spot on the bathroom rota for the next YEAR.

Rose

You're the best. Thank you both. See you Saturday. I can't believe we're going to try this. I hope Maltie approves.

Otto

He's still your pony for now. Good luck!

Saddling up Maltie bright and early on Saturday morning with butterflies in her stomach, Rose knew this time luck would not be enough. She tried to tell herself they were only going out on a trail, like the ones they'd done on holiday. But it felt very, very different to be doing it on her own. Should she give up on the idea and let Maltie go straight to Lavinia?

"You're here early." Carolyn looked over the stable door and made her jump. "Last ride out with him, is it? I'm sorry Rose. That's tough."

Rose nodded, not trusting herself to speak.

"I feel bad that I encouraged you to go on that holiday. This would be easier if you hadn't started to enjoy riding, wouldn't it?"

"Don't feel bad; it was a good thing. The best thing. Thanks Carolyn," she managed. She had a letter in her pocket for Carolyn, which she was planning

to sneak into the lesson register for her to find later. It matched the letter she'd left for her parents. She felt horribly guilty.

"Enjoy the early morning sunshine.

Best time of the day for a ride out." Carolyn waved.

Rose led Maltie into the yard and swung herself up into the saddle, and they walked out of the stables. There was a long way to go to reach London in time.

Plum Orchard Riding Stables and Rose's home were in a commuter village not too many miles from the very outskirts of London, but they needed to ride further into the city to get to the right place and meet Otto and Mei.

The route was straightforward to start with, following a river towpath, like on Rose and Maltie's first hack out on holiday. This path wasn't muddy but Rose had no intention of risking a canter today. She needed Maltie to arrive in tip-top condition. The landscape gradually became more urban, with warehouses and industrial units cropping up on either side of the river, and tower blocks distantly visible. Rose used her phone to find where they needed to leave the towpath and get onto the road. She'd tried to plot a route that took them through parks as much as possible, avoiding any really busy highways.

Not that Maltie cared about traffic. As the route got busier and they started to pass more people, he became bouncy with show-off happiness. Everyone stared at the unusual sight of a pony on the city streets. Whenever anyone actually recognised him Maltie was delighted. He carried his head high and arched his neck, peeking out from under his eyelashes approvingly at anyone paying him a compliment.

"Should never have ratted you out for that rat

mate," yelled a man out of the window of his white van, giving Rose a big thumbs up.

"MD Cheeky made me pukey," agreed a cyclist, overtaking both of them.

Pointing pedestrians, hooting horns and jingle singers made Rose and Maltie's progress slower than planned.

"Sorry: London traffic is terrible," called Rose as she and Maltie clattered round the final corner and spotted Mei and Otto waiting on a wall. "We should have taken the tube."

Mei didn't bother with hello. She held up a plastic bag and shook its contents. "We're going to need to work fast now. I haven't got long before I have to meet my mum."

"I was starting to wonder whether you'd make it Rose. That's the place," said Otto, pointing to a flashy glass-and-chrome office block on the other side of the road. "And this is my brother Harrison. One of my brothers, anyway."

"The biggest: the original and the best." A man further along the wall, who looked disturbingly

like Otto with a beard, glanced up from his phone and waved at Rose. "Pleased to meet you.

Horse emergency I hear? Trailer's a few streets away but parking's costing me a fortune. Otto will pay me back, won't you Otto?" He raised his eyebrows meaningfully at his little brother.

"It's SO kind of you to come and help. I'll find a way to pay you all back, whatever happens." Rose felt like she might cry again. Luckily Mei interrupted before she could get any more emotional.

"Yeah yeah... Ready?"

"Ready," agreed Rose, dismounting. They got to work on Maltie.

CHAPTER EIGHTEEN

"Mackerel Sky Studios, can I help you?" The woman on reception in the chrome-and-glass building did not look up from her sudoku puzzle.

"We've come to see Jole— Jo-Jo McCormack and her manager Bobby Stanley. I think they're recording here?" Otto used his most charming voice.

The woman scanned a list in front of her. "Been here all week. Are they expecting you?"

"Yes," said Rose, crossing her fingers. "All of us," she added.

The woman looked up now. Her mouth dropped. Maltie Delight stood on the marble floor in front of her. He'd been given a quick but thorough makeover by Mei. His mane now had multicolour stripes and he

was also wearing a stuck-on unicorn horn, for maximum impact.

Maltie loved the new additions. He blew out his nostrils and swung his rainbow locks around for the benefit of the woman. He practically winked.

The woman's mouth opened and shut like a goldfish's, but no sound came out. She eventually managed, "Is that a..."

"Former breakfast cereal star turned part-time unicorn?" Mei finished for her. "How clever of you – well recognised! Maltie Delight would love to stop for a photo with you later but right now we'll just head for the studio. Remind us where it is again?"

"Fourth floor... Hang on, you can't just go up." The woman looked alarmed as they started towards the shiny lift opposite the reception desk. "I need to ring. What did you say your names were?"

"No worries, we can introduce ourselves," called Mei.

"Thanks so much."

"Stop! Come back! I'm calling Security..." The lift doors closed. The woman was too late.

"You're so brave Mei. I was ready to run straight back out again," said Rose as they went up in the lift.

"That would have been really stupid given the effort you've put into bringing Maltie here," said Mei. "We won't have long though. Have you thought about what you're going to say when we find them?"

"Sort of..." said Rose. She'd been practising for days.

Maltie was in heaven in the lift. Every surface was spotless and shiny and reflected his beautiful new rainbow hairdo from every possible angle. He snorted and stared at his gorgeous face. Mei and Rose had also taken inspiration from Jonny's donkeys and festooned Maltie's bridle with stick-on gems and fresh flowers. When he shook his head it rained petals.

The lift stopped but it took some time to persuade Maltie to leave the mirrored cubicle.

"Come ON Maltie. This way. We need to find Jolene and Bobby." Rose looked around in panic.

"Oh no. Which one do you think they're in?"

A long corridor of solid oak doors stretched in front of them. Some of them had red "Recording" lights above them. Unfortunately there were no signs to show which one Jolene was behind.

Otto shrugged. "We'll just have to try them all. Here goes..." He squared his shoulders, took a deep breath, plastered a smile on his face and pushed open the first door. A pile of mops and brooms fell out.

"Should I take one of those to sweep up the petals?" Rose looked at the mess her unicorn was leaving in the corridor.

"There are worse things he could be leaving a trail of," pointed out Otto.

Mei tried the next door. There was a horrible discordant squeaking noise as she opened it, and it wasn't from the hinges. An angry looking string quartet raised their bows.

Mei held up a hand in apology. "Just trying to find the right place for our unicorn. I don't think this is it." She shut the door gently.

"This one's the toilet," said Rose as she peeked

round the third door. "I might need to use it actually."
She clutched at her belly, which was churning with
nerves, but Maltie had already nosed open the next
door along. He disappeared inside. "Oh, perhaps
clever Maltie's sniffed out Jolene like a bloodhound!"
Rose clapped her hands. She followed her pony into
the studio.

"Oh no. He hasn't," she corrected, as she saw not a
red-haired singer behind the microphone, but a man in
a baseball cap and low-slung trousers. He was mid-rap.

"Call me Mr Skywalker, yeah I'm harnessing the
force while you're sitting on the night bus eating
chicken and hot... horse?"

"Really sorry to interrupt..." Rose hauled on Maltie's
bridle to get him back out. "Stop that – that's not good
behaviour Maltie!"

Maltie was baring his teeth at the rapper, his ears
pushed right back. The pony had clearly made a
connection between the style of music and his lost
breakfast cereal job. He swung out his front leg and
sent the microphone clattering to the floor.

"Maltie! This man is NOT MD Cheeky," said Rose.

"Hey! You're not just any unicorn. You're Maltie Delight! I used to love your ad!" The rapper grinned, ignoring both his broken microphone and Maltie's threatening teeth. "Ah, that animated rat wannabe is no friend of mine. You own your rage my brother. You were robbed."

The man held out his fist to bump Maltie's shoulder and then reached into his pocket for an extra-strong mint. After a moment's hesitation the pony lowered his lips and accepted this peace offering.

"So you think my work sounds like MD Cheeky?" The rapper shook his head sorrowfully. He turned to a tired-looking woman wearing headphones behind a mixing desk. "Book out this studio for another week Ange and throw away the first cut. We're starting again from the beginning."

The woman sank her head into her hands. Maltie came out of the room without jibbing now; he could recognise a fellow artist needing creative space.

"This is even harder than I thought," said Mei in the corridor.

"At least there's only a few more it could be," said Otto, looking at the last doors.

"I don't think we're going to get the chance to try them," said Rose, looking back over her shoulder. The lift doors were opening. A man in uniform stepped out: Security had caught up with them.

"You! Stop right there!" the man shouted. "Put your hooves up and no funny business with that horn."

He advanced towards the four of them with his hands outstretched, making a pointing gun shape. Halfway down the corridor he realised he was looking a bit silly and dropped his arms to his side. He tried to regain some authority. "The police have been called and they're on their way to arrest you."

"But we haven't done anything!" said Otto reasonably. "We're only trying to talk to Jo-Jo."

"We'd have been in and out already if you'd put signs on these doors. It's very confusing," said Mei. "If only I'd brought my lasso we could tie him up," she added in a quieter voice to Otto and Rose.

"This is all my fault," muttered Rose. What had she been thinking of, coming here? She relaxed her hold on the rope and twined her fingers round Maltie's silky mane, but he slipped out of her grasp. His attention had been caught by the glint of the lift doors reopening. He wanted another go in the special shiny space – it had been several minutes since he'd last had the chance to admire himself. He trotted happily back down the corridor towards the guard.

"Stay where you are! I'm warning you..." The security guard pressed himself against the wall as Maltie approached. Rose felt a pang of sympathy: this guard obviously found ponies as alarming as she once had. The poor man needed to spend more time around them.

"This is your last chance to stop!" he said.

But Maltie kept going. As he brushed past the guard, the man panicked, threw out his arm and smashed the glass of the fire alarm on the wall next to him.

All around them doors flew open and musicians of all types plunged out into the corridor.

Over the racket of the alarm, Rose heard a familiar husky voice behind her.

"Hello Maltie."

They'd found Jolene at last.

CHAPTER NINETEEN

The fire alarm still ringing, all the occupants of Mackerel Sky Studios were ushered out of the building and crowded into a concrete car park out the back. Rose, Maltie Delight, Otto and Mei found themselves jostling for space among bewildered musicians and their instruments, angry music producers and startled office staff clutching mugs of coffee. Fire engines and police cars with flashing blue lights and blaring sirens began to arrive.

This was not the way Rose had dreamed of making her appeal to Jolene and Bobby; not how she had practised her pitch. Old Rose wanted to push her way out of the throng, start running and not stop until she was safe at home. But new Rose had Mei and Otto standing at her shoulders in solidarity. And new Rose, now Rose, was also holding a pony she loved with all her heart. If she wanted to have any chance of keeping him, there could be no running.

She turned and pushed her way through the crowd to where Jolene and Bobby were standing. The singer and her manager were blinking and dishevelled. It looked like they hadn't been outside for days. An important-looking man in a suit and sunglasses was standing beside them drumming his fingers impatiently. He looked at Maltie without recognition.

"This interruption some kind of set-up?" he snapped. "Do you know this unicorn Jo-Jo?"

Jolene nodded to Rose and smiled wearily at Maltie. "Two of a kind, this pony and me. Both still chasing the end of our rainbows." She reached out and stroked his multi-coloured mane as it fluttered in the breeze. "Nice dye job," she said to Rose.

"I hope I got it right this time and it's the sort that will wash straight out but I'm not sure..." Rose began.

Mei gave her a sharp elbow. "Get on with it! The firefighters are coming back out and that security guard's pointing us out to the police!"

Rose bit her lip and started again. She turned to Bobby with determination. "My Maltie's probably got to be sold, but I thought I'd bring him to see you both first. Just in case … I mean I wondered whether you could … whether you might want to …" she gulped, "… hire him to use on your album for promotion?"

Bobby didn't meet her eye. Rose felt herself flush red but forced herself to continue. "You mentioned something about it when we were camping? You took his photo lots. And I thought that … Maltie's good at promoting things… He really likes… I thought you could…"

Bobby's face was discouraging. Rose ran out of steam.

"Hmph," the important-looking man broke in. "Promoting their album? What album? I don't know who you are but I'm the MD of Mackerel Sky, and I can tell you there's not going to be an album at this rate lovey. They've been here all week trying to find the magic of the rough cut that got Jo-Jo studio time. I'm sorry Bobby, but I think this break has come at a good time. We need to call it a day."

Rose stared at the three of them in dismay. She'd gone to all this effort for nothing? To top it all off it looked as though they were about to be arrested. She hoped the police wouldn't lock Maltie up; he wouldn't approve of a cell. Would Lavinia still buy him if he came with a criminal record?

"Give Jo-Jo one more take when we go back upstairs Sanjay," Bobby pleaded. "We'll find it this time."

"We've run out of time. It was a nice idea to try and bring Jo-Jo back, but I'm sorry both, I've not been feeling it. The contract offer's off." The man turned to go.

The alarm was also off now. People were starting to go back into the building.

"Wait!" Jolene said, and her voice had the command of someone who has played stadiums. While the two men had been arguing she'd been communing with Maltie Delight, stroking him and staring into his eyes. "It's been a difficult few weeks, what with splitting from Billy and moving back here. I've been out of the studio too long and it always takes me a while to get my groove without an audience. But something about this pony's journey speaks to me." She plucked a flower from Maltie's headband, sniffed its perfume then stuck it behind her ear. "Now I'm ready," she said, and she straightened her shoulders and took a deep breath.

In the car park, over a backing track of sirens, traffic and the disgruntled chat of the crowd, Jolene began to sing. As so many others had before, she sang to Maltie Delight, but this was not a breakfast cereal jingle. It was a poignant song about lost love and lost fame and lost youth, with a sprinkling of rhinestones. As her powerful voice soared, the crowd in the car park hushed. They stopped shuffling back to the building and turned to watch, aware that they were being treated to something special. All the sirens were switched off. Police and firefighters with tears welling in their eyes removed their helmets in respect. Maltie put his head to one side and whickered softly.

Jolene hit the chorus for a second time. Gaining confidence from her audience now she changed tempo. Her song became upbeat and her melody was infectious: first a saxophonist, then a guitarist and then a double bassist got out their instruments and started to play along. And as they picked up the tune, others followed.

It became a free-for-all jam. A girl group hummed backing vocals and a trio of firefighters with deep bass voices joined them. Two drummers took sticks out of their pockets and riffed a rhythm on the bonnet of the fire engine. The string quartet struck up, sounding much better than the original music they'd been recording. Maltie's new rapper friend cupped his hands together and beat-boxed. Even the security guard grabbed a pair of spoons and slapped them enthusiastically against his leg.

Everyone was dancing too – even Maltie swished his tail and nodded his head. Some people climbed on top of the police cars to throw their best moves, and some of those people were the police. The whole car park swayed, jumped and jiggled to Jolene's tune.

When the song came to an end there was whooping and cheering and hugs and back-slapping. Maltie Delight tossed his mane, stamped his feet and whinnied and everyone laughed.

Bobby punched the air. "What a fusion! That's the pot of gold at the end of the rainbow right there. You feel that Sanjay?"

Sanjay whipped off his sunglasses and smiled broadly at last. "Sensational Jo-Jo; welcome back. Come inside and we'll lay down that track before you lose the momentum. Hmmm..." He looked around at all the other musicians thoughtfully. "I think we're going to need a bigger studio." He turned to Maltie. "Good work unicorn. Remind me to stand you a round of oats one day."

Jolene bestowed a kiss on Maltie's forehead, ruffled Rose's hair, then she and Bobby and everyone else followed Sanjay inside. The last to leave were the police and firefighters, who seemed rather reluctant to put their helmets back on, get into their vehicles and drive away.

Rose, Mei, Otto and Maltie found themselves alone in the car park.

"That went unexpectedly well," said Mei. "But are they not going to come back with a cheque book?"

Rose hugged Maltie sadly. "They didn't mention money. I suppose that's the end of that brilliant idea."

"It's great that you tried," said Otto. "At least we helped Jolene find her music again. You never know, something may still come of that."

"Even if it does it'll be too late. We'd better go home and let Lavinia take Maltie tomorrow," said Rose, turning her face and burying it in her pony's soft pink neck so no one could see her tears.

"I'll go and find Harrison and bring the trailer," said Otto tactfully.

"I'll ring my mum," said Mei.

They slunk away to give Rose and Maltie some space. But as they disappeared, two other people arrived at the car park entrance. They spotted Rose and started running.

"ROSE!"

Rose turned to face her furious parents. She wondered if being arrested might have been the better option.

CHAPTER TWENTY

"What were you thinking riding all this way on your own?"

"We've been frantic!"

"You're still only a beginner Rose! Coming into the city with him – do you have ANY idea how dangerous that was?"

"You could have fallen into a ditch. He could have bolted down a dual carriageway. You could have got lost or injured in a million different ways. You could have died!"

Rose looked at her riding boots. "We were fine. Maltie looked after me and I looked after him. We've got good at that. I mean, it wasn't as dangerous as the time we nearly fell off a cliff in the fog…" Rose glanced at her parents' scarlet faces and thought it might be better not to continue that story. "I'm sorry. I didn't know what else to do." She took a deep breath. "I know I'm a disappointment to you."

There was a silence. Rose's parents looked at each other. Then her dad spoke, even more fiercely than before. "A disappointment? Rose you frightened us, you really frightened us, but how could you think you disappoint us? We are the luckiest lucky parents in the world to have you as our daughter."

"I don't think so. I disappoint myself. There's lots of things I've never been any good at," said Rose in a small voice. "I don't get invited to parties and then I hide in the bathroom at the ones I am invited to. I always get picked last for teams. And I got moved down a set in Maths. And remember that time I forgot my words and ran off stage at the carol concert?"

"We're the luckiest lucky parents in the universe Rose," her mum echoed. "The only disappointment is that you didn't feel you could talk to us about all of this."

"I'm sorry," Rose said again. "It was just..." She

looked across at her wannabe unicorn and sighed. "…Maltie. He's so sure he's good at everything he made me feel maybe I could do some things."

"You love him," said her mum gently.

Rose nodded sadly. "It's OK. I'll get over it. It was a daft idea to bring him here."

"It was very daft," said her mum. "And it was gutsy. You've been brave Rose, really brave."

"Love, in my experience, isn't something you 'get over'," said her dad, looking at her mum.

"Nor in mine," agreed Rose's mum. "Rose: two things. One, you must promise never, ever to pull a stunt like this again."

"I won't," said Rose. It was pretty unlikely that she would ever need to ride a unicorn to London to try to secure him a music promotion job again.

"And two, whatever happens and however we manage it, we are not selling Maltie Delight."

"But…" began Rose. "I don't want… I can't let you…"

"We're a family Rose. And we should have realised Maltie is part of our family now. Whatever it costs, I'll work something out with Miss Pickford."

Rose couldn't speak. She hugged her parents and then threw her arms around Maltie's neck. He accepted her affection but twisted away slightly.
He'd discovered he could see his reflection in the tinted windows of the studio building and he didn't want his sightline blocked.

"Maltie!" whispered Rose. Her stomach somersaulted. Wouldn't Maltie still prefer to go to Lavinia? Shouldn't her parents spend their money on something else? Was she just being selfish? But as her unicorn turned his head at her voice and blew

out his nostrils softly, Rose decided she didn't need to think about Lavinia any more. Maltie belonged to her.

* * *

"Marshmallow sandwich?" Otto placed a perfectly toasted gooey ball between two chocolate digestives and held it out.

"Ah go on then." Mei practically snatched it out of his hand.

"I'll have another in a bit once some space opens up inside," said Rose. "I'm kind of stuffed. Your camp catering's a LOT better than Billy's."

"Thanks," said Otto. "I was pretty proud of that cheesy bread. I had to knead it and everything. Not to mention protect it while it was cooling in the kitchen from everyone else who wanted to eat it."

"Home-made baked beans too! Who knew how good they'd be?!"

"Mum did those," admitted Otto. "They didn't look hard so I'll learn how to do it for next time. Talking of beans, have you heard how Billy's getting on in Arizona?"

"He's good, I think. Jo-Jo's been in touch with him. They're getting on better now they're in different continents. He sent her a postcard that said he was off to a rodeo." Rose remembered the last rodeo Billy had attempted. "Hope he's just watching it…"

"His next postcard will be from a hospital bed," said Mei. "And it's 'Jo-Jo', is it? She your best friend now that song's being played everywhere?"

"No, I've already got two best friends." Rose smiled shyly at Otto and Mei. "But I do have a bit of an announcement. Maltie is going to be back up on a billboard soon. I took him to do a cover shoot for Jo-Jo's album last weekend. She told the record company he had to be on it."

"No WAY – that's brilliant!" said Otto. "So our plan did work in the end? I bet Maltie loved being back in a studio."

"He was pretty happy to have a professional doing his hair again," admitted Rose.

"How much did they pay?" asked Mei, ever practical.

"Enough to make me feel better about Mum and Dad's contribution to Maltie's costs. Miss Pickford has been letting us pay off our debt slowly anyway – Mum negotiated that. She and Miss Pickford had a proper meeting and shouted at each other for a bit and then stopped and found that they actually got on well. They're friends now: it's terrifying!" Rose shook her head in wonder. "I've also come up with another way to earn money. Maltie was so patient with children when we were with the donkeys…"

"You're sending him down to work the beach for Jonny?" interrupted Otto, startled.

"No," Rose said. "I'm going to dress him up as a unicorn for little kids' pony parties at Plum Orchard. They can groom him and I'll lead them out on rides. I've got myself fairy wings to wear. We've got our first booking next weekend."

"Oh brilliant. Maltie will love that. Clever you," said Otto.

Rose was about to shake her head modestly but then decided she agreed with Otto: she was a bit clever and brilliant.

"At least Dougal and Pepper keep Maltie's hooves on the ground," said Otto, looking over to where their ponies were grazing together in the soft evening light.

Rose could see that Maltie had some tangles in his mane and even some mud splatters on his legs but, like a film star enjoying being in their pyjamas in private, he didn't seem to mind. "I think he likes hanging out with them more than doing a photo shoot. Even Maltie needs to be an ordinary pony sometimes."

They had another round of marshmallow sandwiches and lay back watching the stars, feeling

warm and sleepy from the food and fire. The sound
of one of Otto's brothers playing the guitar came from
the cottage. Rose's eyes closed. She was almost asleep
when she felt hair tickling her face and warm wet lips
nibbling her cheek.

"Maltie's giving you a kiss," said Mei.

"Or licking off marshmallow," said Rose. She sat

up and stroked her beautiful pony's nose and smiled at him.

Mei nudged Otto sharply in the ribs. "Go on!" she hissed.

Otto gave a small cough. "So Rose," he said. "Now that you're here enjoying my fabulous hospitality and we've helped you keep Maltie, and given that we're your very best friends…"

"Yes…" Rose narrowed her eyes suspiciously. "What do you want?"

"It's time you told us," said Mei. "We need to know."

"What?" asked Rose again.

"What your prize-winning slogan was of course," said Otto. "Just how did you win Maltie Delight?"

"Oh!" said Rose. She reddened in the darkness. "You know, it wasn't any good. I'm pretty sure they never bothered to read them all and I just got picked out of a hat. I don't even know if I remember what—"

"TELL US," said Mei.

There was no escape.

"I'd like to win Maltie Delight because…" Rose gulped, "…it will be a mag-NEIGH-ficent adventure."

There was silence. Even the distant guitar music had stopped.

"Wow," said Mei. "That's awful Rose."

"Really, really bad," agreed Otto.

"I know," said Rose. She smiled at her pony in perfect happiness. "What can I say? I was very, very lucky!"